"Not that I'm not glad to see you," Logan said, **"but what are you doing here?"**

"I've come to take you away from all this. I'm kidnapping you." T.S. gave him one of the dazzling smiles he was rapidly coming to crave.

A smile flirted with his mouth too. "And just how are you planning to do that, Ms. Winslow?"

Without breaking eye contact, T.S., slowly inched off the black marble-topped desk. She bent down to drape her arms around his shoulders. "I'm going to tell you I missed you today," she whispered, sliding her hands up to caress the back of his neck.

A shiver of anticipation ran through him. "Is that all?"

"Then I'm going to tell you I want you. Don't you think we've waited long enough?"

He sat very still, mesmerized by the sound of her voice and the sight of her moistened lips. "And if that doesn't work?"

"I'm going to kiss you until you give in. . . ."

WHAT ARE *LOVESWEPT* ROMANCES?

They are stories of true romance and touching emotion. We believe those two very important ingredients are constants in our highly sensual and very believable stories in the *LOVESWEPT* line. Our goal is to give you, the reader, stories of consistently high quality that may sometimes make you laugh, sometimes make you cry, but are always fresh and creative and contain many delightful surprises within their pages.

Most romance fans read an enormous number of books. Those they truly love, they keep. Others may be traded with friends and soon forgotten. We hope that each *LOVESWEPT* romance will be a treasure—a "keeper." We will always try to publish

LOVE STORIES YOU'LL NEVER FORGET
BY AUTHORS YOU'LL ALWAYS REMEMBER

The Editors

Loveswept® 545

Theresa Gladden
T.S., I Love You

BANTAM BOOKS
NEW YORK · TORONTO · LONDON · SYDNEY · AUCKLAND

T.S., I LOVE YOU

A Bantam Book / May 1992

If you would be interested in receiving protective vinyl
covers for your Loveswept books, please write to this address
for information:

> *Loveswept*
> *Bantam Books*
> *P.O. Box 985*
> *Hicksville, NY 11802*

ISBN 0-553-44177-9

Published simultaneously in the United States and Canada

PRINTED IN THE UNITED STATES OF AMERICA

OPM   0 9 8 7 6 5 4 3 2 1

Do ye hear the children weeping . . .
Oh my brothers, they are weeping bitterly,
They are weeping in the playtime of the others.

—ELIZABETH BARRETT BROWNING

This story is dedicated to all the Jesses. May they find shelter and hope, and weep no more in the playtime of others.

And to Kathy Guzzo and Lisa Cantrell, both gentle true spirits and lifelong friends.

Acknowledgments

The author commends Bobby Stewart for his work with the youth of Rockingham County, North Carolina, and she is grateful for his expert advice on juvenile justice.

One

June 1977

She was alone. It was obvious no one was coming to claim her. Except maybe, Moon Man Chase thought as his gaze strayed to the bus-terminal newsstand, the human vulture who hungrily eyed the girl with the delicate face and hair the color of flame curling down to her waist.

Moon Man folded his Richmond, Virginia, street map. In the month since he had run away from the commune founded by his parents, he had gained enough experience to recognize another kid on the run. He had also learned to identify the flesh peddlers and freaks who preyed on runaways.

He stuffed the map in his jeans and sank a little deeper in the shadow of the lockers. It was time to split, but he was reluctant to move.

Once again, his gaze was drawn to the girl. She couldn't be more than sixteen, like himself. Dressed in a pink-and-white blouse and skirt, she sat gazing around her like a bewildered princess who had just escaped her ivory tower and didn't know what to do with her freedom. She looked confused, lost, and about as able to fend for herself as the newborn lambs he used to raise on Freedom Farm.

Forget her. Moon Man impatiently tossed his long blond hair out of his eyes and readjusted his backpack. Her problems were none of his business. He had his own to deal with.

But the girl's innocence bothered him. It radiated from her like a beacon on a pitch-black night. He knew she wouldn't last two minutes alone on the street. If nothing else, he had to warn her about freaks who victimized young girls.

One glance at the newsstand told him a simple warning wasn't going to be enough. The vulture was moving in for the kill, and he was closer than Moon Man. Wishing he'd never seen the girl, Moon Man headed toward her.

The predator reached her first. "You all alone, honey?" He bent down and laid a hand on her knee. "The name's Flash, and, baby, you look like you need a friend." With his other hand he reached for her suitcase and purse.

"I—I'm waiting for someone," she stammered, shrinking away from him.

"Sure, honey, and here I am. Friend Flash will take real good care of you." He latched on to her elbow and pulled her to her feet.

"Please go away. I told you I'm waiting for—" She hesitated, then blurted out, "My aunt. She'll be here any minute."

"I don't think she wants you for a friend," Moon Man said, coming to a halt just behind the freak.

Flash turned to glare at him. "Back off, hippie boy. This ain't none of your business." An oil-slicked smile twisted his lips. "Hey, I know some people who'd be real interested in getting to know a pretty blond boy like you."

Eyes taking on a thermonuclear freeze, Moon Man curled his fingers into his palms. The piece of scum outweighed him by at least a hundred pounds and was a good six inches taller. If it came down to a fight, he would lose.

He locked gazes with the girl. A plea for his help shimmered along with fear in her tragic, deep blue eyes. He forced his lips into what he hoped was a reassuring smile as he racked his brain for a way to create a diversion.

"There's a couple of cops over at the snack bar," he told her, though it was a lie. "Between the two of us, we can make enough noise to get their attention. Bet they'd love to crack a billy club over this lowlife's head." Glancing at Flash, he added with a nonchalance he was far from feeling, "I saw a man get his skull cracked at the Democratic Convention in Chicago in '68. It wasn't a pretty sight."

Flash looked nervously over his shoulder. He was distracted just long enough for Moon Man to drive a fist into his soft stomach. The blow doubled him over. He let go of the girl's arm.

Moon Man grabbed her hand. "Run," he hissed, pulling her along.

"My purse!" The girl dragged her feet. "He's got all my money." Her voice rose to a panicked squeak. "Aren't you going to do something?"

"Forget it." Adrenaline pumped through Moon Man's veins as he kept going. "Stay or come with me. I don't care."

Not waiting for an answer, he shook off her hand and spun toward the nearest street exit. Uncertain whether it made him feel better or worse, he soon heard her sandals pounding on the floor behind him.

Seconds later, Moon Man shoved his way outside. Hot, humid air and exhaust fumes filled his nose and lungs. He raced down the sidewalk, looking for a place to hide.

Darting a glance over his shoulder, he saw the girl was still with him, maybe a yard back. Suddenly, she stumbled. He saw her going down, as if in slow motion, arms flung out in front of her to break her fall. His first instinct was to keep going. But something about her innocence and tragic eyes had touched his angry heart.

Moon Man swore silently, then turned and sprinted back.

She was still on her knees when he reached her. "Go on." Her breath came in panicked little gasps, and her face was deathly white. "I—I can't—can't—"

"Yes, you can. On your feet, princess." He looped his arm around her waist and pulled her up, then looked back at the bus station. "Here comes your friend Flash. He's looking the other way. Move it. *Now!*"

He quickly led her into the recessed entrance of the nearest building. He tried the door. Locked. He pressed his back into the shadows, making himself as small as possible.

"I'm scared," she whispered, clutching his shirt.

"So am I." Instinctively, he put his arms around her. When she buried her face against his neck, the scent of her perfume reminded him of home. She smelled like the spring flowers and spices his mother dried and kept in pottery bowls throughout the communal living quarters. Feeling a violent tremor rip through her, he tightened his arms protectively around her.

As the sound of footsteps neared, his heart began to beat so loudly, he feared it would lead the vulture right to them. So close, he silently raged, he'd come so close to being reborn. The anger in his soul grew. He envisioned all his dreams blowing away like ashes in the wind.

Moon Man Chase had never prayed in his life. He decided now was as good a time as any to start.

Oh please, T.S. Winslow silently implored. *Please, God, make us invisible.* She prayed that awful man would look right through them—the way her father looked at her without seeming to notice or care if she was really there.

Desperately, she counted the seconds between footfalls. The comforting distraction her mother had taught her to help conquer her fear of lightning and explosive thunder did little to quell the terror mounting inside her.

The heavy sound of footsteps grew closer. She swallowed the scream welling up in her throat.

Half a minute later T.S. hardly dared to breathe as the man ran past them. Still shivering, she raised her head to find her own disbelief mirrored in the boy's eyes. "Is he gone?"

"I think so. Stay here." The boy released her and went to check the street. He signaled for her to join him. "See that black car? We're going to—"

"We're not going to steal it!" she squeaked.

"Would you let me finish a sentence before you jump to conclusions?" he said, the words rife with irritation. "I've never stolen anything, and I don't plan to pick up the habit now. Just follow me." He took off running.

T.S. didn't hesitate to go after the boy. She kept close behind him, dodging, darting, ducking, copying his every move. Three blocks away from the bus station, he finally slowed down.

"What's your name?" she called out. "Could we rest for a minute?"

Not bothering to answer, he slipped into the narrow opening between two deserted-looking buildings.

She followed him, but came to a halt at the mouth of the blind alley, warily eyeing the trash piled high against dirty brick walls. Nothing in her upbringing had prepared her for a place like this. Sighing, she delicately picked her way through the litter. Her nose wrinkled at the smell of foul garbage and other odors she didn't care to identify. Suddenly, she stopped, a look of horror on her face.

"What's the matter, princess? Find a rat?" Moon Man called from the far end of the alley where he was sitting on a wooden crate.

One hand over her heart, the other pointing to a cardboard box, she gasped out, "That man. I think he's dead!"

"What makes you think he's dead?"

"He looks dead," she said indignantly.

Moon Man took out the street map. "It's probably just some old guy sleeping off a snootful." As he spread out the map, he heard a loud, grunting snore that proved him right. "Doesn't sound dead to me," he just had to say.

T.S. sat down beside the boy, distressed by the plight of the poor man. "Why doesn't he go home to sleep?"

Moon Man frowned at her, as if annoyed she even had to ask. "Probably because he doesn't have one."

Realistically, T.S. knew there were "underprivileged" people in the world, but she had never imagined them living in a dirty alley with only cardboard for shelter. Tears welled up in her eyes as she realized how terribly inadequate it was to give old clothes and baskets of fruit to the needy at Christmas.

Wanting to know what a "snootful" was, she turned to the boy. His attention was on the map, and she decided it wouldn't be wise to disturb him. Folding her hands politely, she studied him while waiting for him to finish.

He was only a couple of inches taller than she, and she considered herself on the short side at five foot three. She glanced down at his large feet and thought about how he moved with a restless, energetic grace. He would probably grow into those feet, she decided, the way a puppy grows into its paws.

Her gaze traveled back up, taking in his jeans, oversized shirt with a blue peace sign on the back, and straight golden hair she'd die to have. His profile held the promise of strength and power. She liked his square-jawed face, even though it was a little too thin and his mouth looked as though it had to work hard for a smile. He had the kind of blue eyes that could freeze nerves with a single glance. Yet the way he had looked at her back at the bus station had made her feel safe and warm inside.

Altogether, she found him sort of dangerous and exciting at the same time. On the outside he seemed hard, but since he'd bothered to help her at all, she suspected he might be very different inside.

Unable to stand the silence any longer, she said, "My name is Tyler Scott Winslow the Fourth. Isn't that an awful name for a girl? My father's the Third, you see, and he wanted a boy to carry on the family name. I'm an only child, so I got stuck with it. Everyone calls me T.S." She paused for breath and smiled brightly. "And you are?"

"Moon Man Chase." He tensed, waiting for the derision he'd learned to expect.

"Moon Man Chase," she repeated softly. "How lovely. It sounds so poetic."

A surprised ghost of a smile tugged at his lips, but he quickly subdued it. A long time ago the Music Maker had told him, "Never let 'em see you sweat, boy. Never let 'em see you hurting. Keep your feelings on the inside." It wasn't a philosophy Sean and Summer, his parents, agreed with. But it had become Moon Man's way of coping with the world outside Freedom Farm.

"What's a snootful?" T.S. asked. "Did you really see a man get his skull cracked?"

"Drunk. Yes, I did."

"Oh." She nodded. "Mr. Oxford imbibes too much at our New Year's Eve parties. My father says he should know better because he's a banker. You don't talk much, do you? How old are you? Weren't you a little young to attend the Democratic Convention?"

He fixed her with a glacial stare. "I'll be seventeen next month. My parents took me there to protest."

Her eyes widened. "I just turned sixteen in May. What were they protesting?"

"The war. Government. Whatever was fashionable." Irritably, he flipped his hair out of his eyes.

"Are your parents radicals? My father's a Republican."

"*Princess*, you ask too many questions." He got up and started walking away.

"Where are we going now?"

"*We?*" He whirled around. "Where were *you* going back at the bus station?"

"I don't know." She looked miserable. "Anywhere the money in my purse would take me, I guess."

Against his will the harsh line of his mouth softened along with his eyes. "Where do you live? Do you know anyone here?"

"In Greensboro, North Carolina. No, I don't know anyone here." She smiled. "Except you, of course."

He looked up at the sky. The last thing he needed was a sad, helpless princess hanging on to his shirttail. Glancing back at her, though, he knew he couldn't abandon her. "You can come with me," he said grudgingly. "I know a guy who'll let us crash at his place for a while. Just don't talk my ear off, okay?"

"Okay." She stood up, smiling sweetly. "I won't be a bit of trouble to you, I promise."

The hell she wouldn't, Moon Man thought, stalking out of the alley. Her blind faith and naiveté had already added another burden to his thin shoulders.

T.S. kept her promise to be quiet for the next hour as they walked through the kind of area she'd only driven through before, with car doors locked and windows rolled up tight. Feeling saddened by the desperation and hopelessness she saw around her, she moved closer to the boy and sneaked her hand into his.

Moon Man made no comment when she took his hand. She was scared and trying to be brave about it. He didn't like the predatory stares they were receiving any more than she did.

The small hand entwined with his suddenly reminded him of Sage, the Rainbow Woman's seven-year-old daughter. So many members of the commune family had left over the past few years. Some of them he missed in his secret heart of hearts, and Sage was one of them. Wherever the little mouse of a girl was now, he hoped she was happy.

The sun had set by the time he hustled T.S. up to an efficiency apartment located over a boisterous corner tavern. He introduced his friend Jack to her, then took the older man out for a talk, leaving T.S. to inspect the sparsely furnished but orderly place. An hour later he returned alone, with their dinner.

After polishing off the last bite of her hamburger, T.S. cheerfully said, "Thank you for rescuing me at the bus station. Wasn't that man awful?"

"You know he was a pimp, don't you?" Moon Man popped a French fry in his mouth. Her puzzled expression told him she didn't have a clue about how close she had come to spending the rest of her life wishing she were dead. "Never mind. I'll explain it some other time."

"I've never been so scared in all my life," she confided, getting up to help him clear the table. "It's the worst thing that's ever happened to me." She followed him into the tiny kitchen. "Except when my mother died," she added in a quivering voice.

The strain of the day's events, the burden of his

companion, and his guilt for having exposed—
however briefly—an innocent like T.S. to Jack,
who was a criminal any way you looked at it,
suddenly evaporated Moon Man's patience. "*Princess*, if that's the worst that's ever happened to
you, then you've led a charmed life. Did Daddy
take the T-bird away? Is that why you left home?"
he asked caustically.

"Stop calling me princess." Her lower lip trembled. "Why do you say it so hatefully?"

"Because you act like one. You're the most
helpless female I've ever met. I don't think you
have any more idea how to get along in the world
than—than—Lord, who let you out of your ivory
tower?"

Her eyes filled with resentment. "Well, pardon
me for living!" Unaccustomed as she was to arguing, it was the most scathing reply she could think
of. "If I annoy you so much, we can go our
separate ways. Right now."

They faced off like two wildcats, eyes locked,
claws bared, lungs fighting for the same air. Tension
crackled between them like static electricity.

Moon Man opened his mouth and quickly closed
it again. It was no use arguing with her. He
doubted even the most lurid details could make a
dent in her wholesome spirit. Given his experience
she was as much an alien being to him as he was
to her. He wondered if they even spoke the same
language.

Tossing his hair out of his eyes, he walked over
to his backpack. "You can use the shower first."
He took out a tie-dyed shirt. "I'm sorry about your
mother."

Blinking back tears, T.S. accepted the shirt
from him and headed for the bathroom. He was

the oddest boy she'd ever met. Prickly as a desert cactus one minute and so kind the next.

After indulging in a very hot shower and a good cry, she opened the door between the two rooms, then stopped to stare at Moon Man. He was making lemonade in the kitchen, wearing only his jeans that rode low on his hips. Her gaze riveted on his naked back. Never having experienced physical desire before, T.S. was unprepared for the dizzy sensation that invaded her mind and limbs.

Hero worship shining in her eyes, she gulped air into her lungs. As she crept closer, she noticed an intriguing birthmark in the shape of a crescent moon high on his right shoulder blade. She smiled. So that was how he'd got his name.

She sifted through the hazy thoughts floating in her head as she stopped beside him. "It was nice of Jack to go stay with his mother, wasn't it?"

Moon Man's mouth formed what might pass for a grin. "I said he's staying with his old lady." Seeing a frown daintily arch her brows, he clarified, "His girlfriend, not his mother."

"Oh." She tried to sit on the counter, jumping and arching backward. After observing her unsuccessful attempts, he grabbed her by the waist and hauled her onto the countertop. There she sat kicking her heels lightly against the cabinet, watching him work and trying not to stare at his body, and listening to him hum "Purple Haze," which was the song currently rising up from the tavern below.

"I like your necklace," she finally said, looking at the crescent moon and stars intricately worked on the silver medallion resting upon his smooth chest.

"Thanks," he said gruffly, remembering all the jokes and insults he'd taken from the kids at school for being a boy who wore a necklace. No one was ever going to laugh at him again for being weird and different, because Moon Man Chase was going to disappear forever.

Jack was going to help him become a regular citizen. *Need a new identity? Jack was your man.* Excitement danced just beneath his skin as he thought about his new life. His first step would be to join the navy and see the world.

"T.S., have you ever seen the ocean?"

She almost fell off the counter in her amazement that he'd actually initiated a conversation. "Oh yes, my mother and I used to spend every summer on the Outer Banks near Kitty Hawk, where the Wright brothers made their first flight. It's so beautiful and peaceful there."

"I saw the ocean once." A glow came into his eyes. "I love it. Everything about it. The sound of the waves. The way it feels, smells, tastes. Someday, I'm going to buy a house at the beach and have the ocean for my front yard."

T.S. smiled. Moon Man smiled back, and for once, she realized he wasn't having to work at it. "I live in a neighborhood no one moves in or out of. You're born there and you die there. Our house is like a museum, filled with things you can't touch. When I have a house of my own, the people in it are going to be more important than *things*. Why are you running away from home?"

He glanced at her, then quickly shuttered his gaze. But not so quickly that she didn't see the sad expression haunting his eyes.

Moon Man didn't know how to explain that he wanted Ozzie and Harriet for parents instead of aging flower children. He wanted to be "one of the guys" instead of the weirdo from the commune up in the hills. He wanted people to look at him with respect, not suspicion, fear, or hatred. He didn't know how to explain the mixture of love and loathing he felt for his parents, and the shame he felt at being one of many to desert Freedom Farm for another life.

Hiding his feelings with sarcasm, he said, "When you don't like the world you're pushed into, you go out and create a new one."

Being a sensitive soul, T.S. recognized the anguish woven into that cryptic statement. She stopped kicking her heels and sat very still. Something was hurting him inside. Hurting him very deeply.

She laid the tips of her fingers on his arm, drawing his attention to her. "I'm sorry."

Tender compassion expressed so simply made Moon Man's throat constrict. He lifted his hand, resting it lightly upon her cheek, and held her gaze until the air he breathed became thicker than clover honey. Unbidden and unwelcome, he began in some unconscious way to understand that T.S. was someone he could love.

His arm dropped back to his side as he looked away. She was a problem he didn't need, but he found he cared about what happened to her. His brooding gaze returned to her. Could he send her home? Would she go? What would she be going back to?

"Were you unhappy at home?" he asked, feeling ill at the thought of anyone treating her cruelly.

She hung her head, hiding behind flame-tinted tresses.

He parted her curtain of hair and raised her

face. A soul-deep dejection was reflected in her eyes. "Is it your father? Can you tell me what he does to you?"

Tears glistened like diamonds on her lashes. "He makes me feel like I'm invisible," she whispered.

Moon Man wrapped his arms around her waist and lifted her down from the counter.

Her hands, trapped between their bodies, formed fists. Tears began to flow in rivulets down her face, and she laid her head upon his shoulder. For the first time since her mother's death, someone held her and comforted her while she cried.

Over the next five days Moon Man grew increasingly alarmed by T.S.'s behavior as she quickly shed what he considered a healthy fear of the neighborhood. Having more than her share of curiosity and compassion, she walked among the paupers, riffraff, and crazies, bestowing her sweet smile on all. If left alone for more than a minute, she was either sneaking food to the nutty old lady who shouted profanities and doom prophesies all day long, or she was trying to befriend and reform Rita, the corner tavern's resident teenage hooker.

Everyone who met T.S. seemed fascinated by her and tolerated her earth-mother ministrations with amused goodwill. But Moon Man constantly worried that her radiant innocence would attract another freak he might not be able to protect her from. He knew he'd better make a decision about what to do with her before she got herself into serious trouble.

What secretly appalled Moon Man the most, though, was his own growing love for her and his overwhelming desire to take her to bed. Sleeping in the same room with her every night was torture. The look of hero worship in her eyes was good for his ego and hell on his hormones. It was only a matter of time before he did something really stupid.

It took Moon Man two more days of internal debate and one phone call to make his decision. It was the right thing to do, he told himself once more as he paid the taxi driver with money borrowed from Jack.

He got out and joined T.S. on the sidewalk in front of the bus terminal.

"I wish you'd tell me where we're going," she complained in her good-natured way.

Answering her with silence, he entwined his fingers with hers and started walking.

The closer they came to the terminal entrance, the more he felt as if someone had filled his sneakers with lead weights. By the time they reached the glass doors, his feet didn't want to move at all.

He stopped. She glanced questioningly up at him. Drawing her to one side, he reached up to touch and then release one of her curls. "Princess, I . . ." He didn't know what to say.

T.S. smiled brightly as she realized he no longer called her princess in a sarcastic tone. Instead, the word was infused with the same warmth she often observed in his gaze.

He swayed toward her, bringing his hands to her shoulders and then to her face. She wondered if he was going to kiss her—something she'd often wished for since their first night together. Eyes open wide and shining, she rested the fingertips of one hand gently, encouragingly, on his cheek.

Turning her head from side to side, he dragged his lips across hers. He drew away for a moment, then laid his mouth upon hers again, touching her with a sweetly probing pressure that parted her lips and allowed him to stroke the softness inside.

His hands dropped to her waist as the kiss became insistent. A spinning sensation urged T.S. to press closer to him. Instinctively, innocently, she moved her body against his in a desire to love and be loved.

Much too soon he lifted his head away from her swelling, burning mouth. He stroked her hair back from her forehead, then captured her trembling fingers in his own for a brief kiss before releasing her.

"I want to give you something," he said in an unsteady voice. He fumbled beneath the neck of his shirt and removed the silver chain. His own hands shook as he placed it over her head and rearranged her hair around it.

Her heart beat furiously. She looked down at the medallion lying between her breasts. Sunlight sparkled on the medallion, seeming to make the crescent moon and stars shine brightly. Her hand closed over it, finding it warm from being nestled against his body. "Thank you. It's so beautiful. I'll wear it always."

He nodded. "It's time to go." His heart was heavy as he led her inside the bus terminal.

A short while later Moon Man came out alone. He walked rapidly, blindly, down the sidewalk. The only thing he could see was the last look of hurt and betrayal in T.S.'s cornflower-blue eyes. He knew it would live in his memory forever.

Two

Sixteen Years Later

The gale hit the Outer Banks off the coast of North Carolina just after sunset. A northeast wind battered the small cottage, making it creak and sigh on its foundation. Rain rattled the windowpanes like a wild thing trying to get in. Wicked lightning streaked through the sky, followed by explosive thunder.

T.S. Winslow sat at the kitchen table in the ocean-front cottage she had rented in Nags Head that morning. She sipped sweet, hot tea in hopes of soothing her nervous reaction to the constant barrage of sound. It wasn't working. Her childhood phobia about storms—the one she thought she had conquered—was back with a vengeance.

Returning to the Outer Banks after all these years might have something to do with the reappearance of her phobia, T.S. mused. She had always loved spending summers with her mother in Southern Shores, a small community just north of Nags Head. This was the first time she had visited the barrier chain of islands since her mother died, and perhaps there were simply too many subconscious emotions tied up with the place and the loss of her beloved mother.

Sighing, she picked up a tube of aloe. Like most fair-skinned redheads, she burned easily, and her short time on the beach that afternoon had produced a slight pinkness on her shoulders, arms, and legs. Her face remained unscathed because she'd remembered to wear a hat.

As T.S. applied the lotion, she prayed the gale wouldn't blow the cottage, with her in it, into the raging Atlantic Ocean. It was hard to believe how fast the storm had moved in. When she'd arrived, not a hint of the impending squall had tainted the water or sky.

Glancing out the window, she saw a jagged bolt of lightning slash through the dark. Her stomach clenched tight. Silently, she counted the seconds, waiting for the frightening break of thunder.

The overhead light flickered. Startled, she dropped the plastic tube on the table. "Take it easy," she murmured, retrieving the lotion and squeezing more onto her palm. "It's only a little storm."

Uh-huh. Sure. The temperature was warm and balmy, but September was still hurricane season. Not the time of year she would willingly have chosen to come here.

To distract herself, T.S. thought about the man she'd driven from Greensboro to Nags Head to find. Logan Hunter owned Hunter Properties, a real estate company that bought, sold, rented, and developed beach property from Corolla to

Hatteras. He'd recently acquired a run-down apartment building in Greensboro that she wanted.

Morally, if not legally, the property belonged to All Saints, she thought with a twinge of indignation. The woman who had owned it had been one of the charity's longtime supporters. She had planned to donate the eight-unit brick apartment house to All Saints, but she had died unexpectedly, with no provision in her will concerning it. It had been left along with the bulk of her estate to her nephew, who had no interest in the organization's work. He had sold the property to Hunter, working it into a larger deal by offering a lower price on some prime beach real estate in exchange for Hunter taking the decrepit apartment building off his hands.

T.S. was determined to buy it. Its proximity to All Saints storefront office made it the perfect location for a temporary shelter for runaway kids, a vital project very close to her heart. She had spent over a year researching, raising money, visiting privately run shelters in other cities, and cutting through local political and bureaucratic red tape.

Now all she had to do was purchase the building, hire the contractors to do the necessary remodeling, and select qualified counselors and volunteers to run the shelter twenty-four hours a day. But first, she had to find Logan Hunter.

A frown creasing her forehead, she went over the scant information she had gathered about the man. Through her connections with the financial network in North Carolina, she had learned a great deal about his assets and business reputation, but everything else was pure speculation. From what she heard, he was into highly lucrative ventures and was considered a tough but fair man to deal with. He possessed an uncanny knack for turning a profit while remaining discreetly out of the limelight. No one seemed to know anything about him on a personal level. In short, he was a mystery man.

Thunder cracked loudly overhead, reminding T.S. of how dangerously close the storm was. Realistically, she knew weatherworn Outer Banks folks would consider this a "puny northeaster." However, the islands were vulnerable to flooding caused by hurricanes and puny northeast gales.

She warily eyed her rented home. It was a relic in that it was one of the few remaining oceanfront cottages *not* built up on piers. The wood-frame house consisted of a living room open to the kitchen, one bedroom, and a bath. It was musty-smelling, drafty, and cheap during the off-season after Labor Day. The best thing about it was the screened-in porch providing a lovely view of the Atlantic Ocean—if one was tall enough to see over the sand dune.

Surely, T.S. rationalized, the cottage's longevity was testimony to its sturdiness. No doubt it had withstood gales that would make this one look tame. But how about flooding?

Storms and floods hadn't been on her mind when she had rented the place that morning. Now she wished she had chosen one of the newer models sitting high up on piers, like the two-story beauty next door.

The relentless wind increased its howling tempo, sending prickles up her spine. The sound of the surf was growing louder, closer, and she found no comfort in knowing only a sand dune stood between her and those angry waves.

She wished Hunter had responded to at least one of her numerous phone messages. If he had, she would be safely curled up on her sofa at home right now.

Her visit to Hunter Properties that morning had proved just as unproductive as her phone calls. His secretary had given her a steely-eyed look and claimed Hunter was indefinitely tied up with an important business matter. T.S. got passed on to a haughty-looking female associate by the name of Melissa, who said she could not speak for Mr. Hunter, nor was she at liberty to discuss the Greensboro property.

Thoroughly annoyed, T.S. had immediately located a rival real estate company and rented this cottage from them. Come hell or high water, she had vowed to remain in Nags Head until the elusive real estate tycoon agreed to talk to her.

She smiled ruefully. Hell and high water were beating on her door a lot sooner than she'd expected. "Wherever you are tonight, Logan Hunter, I hope you're as miserable as I am!"

Why was Hunter so set on avoiding someone he had never met? she wondered as she finished with the aloe. If he was such a hotshot businessman, why was he passing up a potential client?

For weeks she had been plagued with concern that he had secret plans of his own for the building. That would account for his refusal to talk to her. If that was the case, she would just have to convince him to change those plans.

First thing Monday morning she was going to stage an old-fashioned sit-in at Hunter Properties until somebody agreed to discuss business with her. All of the mystery tycoon's agents, the haughty Melissa, and his tank of a secretary combined wouldn't be able to force her to leave. Nothing short of the National Guard bodily removing her from the premises would deter her. Sooner or later, Hunter would at least have to make an appearance to get rid of her.

"Power to the people," she practiced saying, and grinned mischievously as she plucked a shapeless sweatshirt from the back of a rickety chrome-and-vinyl chair. She tugged the shirt over her head, then looked down at herself. If her father could see her attire now, he would die of embarrassment. The neon-green sweatshirt clashed dreadfully with her magenta shorts and socks, but they all were comfortable and bright, which was her preferred fashion. These days, she dressed only to please herself.

An angry flash of lightning made her jump. It was followed by an explosive sound that told her the lightning had found a target. The overhead light flickered once, twice; then the power went out.

T.S. froze in the act of finger-combing her short auburn curls. She wrapped her arms around her stomach, trying to hold back the panic that made her feel physically ill. Her fear of the storm intensified with the thought of being trapped in a frail structure in the dark.

Goose bumps rose on her arms as she listened to the wind and rain pummel the house. She imagined the gale churning up giant waves. Those waves would wash over the dune and come crashing through the wall.

The dark began closing in on her. Maybe the power had gone off only in her cottage. She jumped up. Frantically, she lurched through the kitchen to the living room to look out the window facing the house next door. It was also dark. Her heart sank down to her toes as the contents of her stomach threatened to rise.

She had started to turn away when she noticed a faint amber light flicker on in the second level of the other house. Kerosene lamps, she thought. Earlier, she had seen a tall, distinguished-looking man, dressed in a conservative but beautifully tailored suit, walking up the two flights of stairs to that cottage. Apparently, Mr. Dress-for-Success was better prepared than she for such occurrences. All she had was a flashlight and a very bad case of self-induced fright.

T.S. dug her fingers into her forearms. A crazy notion entered her head. The house next door couldn't be more than a few hundred yards away, and she desperately wanted the comfort of another person and that reassuring glow of light.

Impulsively, she turned and hurried through the room, bumping into furniture in her haste. In the kitchen she rummaged around in a cabinet until she found the flashlight she'd come across that morning. She switched it on and went into the bedroom.

Hastily, she found her tennis shoes and put them on, then grabbed her yellow hooded raincoat from the closet. Her fingers shook as she secured the snaps from knees to chin.

She willed herself to calm down as she retraced her steps, but her will rebelled. Holding the flashlight in a death grip, she stopped at the back door and drew the hood over her head.

Wind shrieked in as she opened the door. Hard pellets of rain stung her legs. Heavy gusts almost forced her back inside, but she pushed forward, fighting to close the door behind her.

Once she was outside, there was nothing to grab on to, and the wind buffeted her to and fro as if she were a Ping-Pong ball. Visibility was poor in the black mat night. The noise of the Atlantic Ocean and shrill wind filled her ears. The scent of salt was heavy in the air.

The road behind the cottage was only a short distance away. By the time she reached it, her sneakers and socks were soaked, weighing her down, making each step more difficult.

She stumbled over a lid that had blown off a metal trash can, and the flashlight flew out of her grasp. She landed hard on her knees and hands. Fragments of shells and crushed rock strewn over the sand bit into her flesh. The shrieking wind swallowed her cry of pain.

Thunder clapped like giant hands overhead. Lightning caught her in the middle of its jagged light, injecting a paralyzing terror through her muscles that quivered like jelly.

She fumbled to retrieve the flashlight, then struggled to her feet. Her heart galloped, speeding the flow of blood through her veins until she was nearly deafened by its pounding rush. The hood slipped back, and her face and hair were immediately drenched. She dragged it back into place and began walking again.

Fear dulled her senses, making her heart hammer against her ribs. Wild thoughts of being struck by lightning almost made her mind shut down. She forced herself to focus on reaching the cottage in front of her. Moving through the solid curtain of rain, she felt as if it were taking her forever to reach the steps leading straight up to the second level.

T.S. realized she was crying as she climbed the

stairs, sometimes on her hands and knees. Her vision spun. The slick surface of the raincoat impeded her progress and provided little protection against the heavy rain and biting wind.

Finally, the last stair was within her grasp. She sobbed in relief as she dropped onto the solid floor of the deck that rose high above the shadow of the sand dune.

She slowly got to her feet and tried to take a few steps. The wind had grown stronger. It caught her in the chest and pushed her backward. The deck handrail stopped her flight. Turning, she grabbed hold of it with both hands.

A streak of lightning filled the sky. In that instant she looked down and saw black waves rolling toward the dune below. She closed her eyes and held on tighter, afraid another gust would send her over the edge, hurling her into the blackness and the angry, echoing boom of the surf.

She forced herself back down onto her hands and knees and inched across the slippery deck. When she reached the door, she pulled herself up by the doorknob, then pounded the flashlight on the solid wood.

A vibrating sound seeped from the house. Her fear-numbed mind sifted through a maze of impressions and identified the driving rhythm of rock music. For one hysterical moment she wondered if she would die beaten by the wind and drowned by the rain, while inside the occupants listened contentedly to Jimi Hendrix grind out "The Star-Spangled Banner."

T.S. added her voice to the pounding. She shouted pleas for help until her throat felt tight and raw.

Suddenly, the doorknob twisted in her hand. The door jerked open. The rapid motion bent her over at the waist, propelling her inside as the door swung inward.

Another gust of wind sent her careening head-first like a human cannonball into the dark silhouette framing the threshold. Grabbing wildly with her hands, she connected with a pair of outstretched arms. Her head butted into a rock-hard stomach. The tackle sent them both stumbling backward into the room.

All she could see were two large bare feet struggling for purchase. Then they were falling. She heard twin groans as she landed in a heap on top of a solidly built masculine body.

For a moment she lay limp, exhausted, and disoriented. The person beneath her panted for air. With her thoughts twisting and distorting, and an electric guitar screeching as Jimi Hendrix sang "Purple Haze," everything took on the surrealistic feel of a Salvador Dalí painting.

Pressing her palms against the carpet, she tried to lever herself up but found she had no strength left in her arms. The man groaned again when she dropped back onto his chest. Inbred politeness and courtesy demanded she apologize. She opened her mouth to speak, and out spilled a disjointed, hoarse patter that made no sense to her whatsoever.

Hands caught her shoulders and shook her slightly. A shower of droplets sprayed in all directions. She shuddered on a ragged breath and became silent.

Again, her mind told her to get up, but her limbs botched the instructions. Soft flesh met the frantic movement of her knee. A very masculine growl assaulted her ears. She went perfectly still.

A second later a deep, pain-filled voice said, "I would very much appreciate it if you'd remove your knee from my groin."

Using what little strength she had left, T.S. rolled to one side and collapsed on the floor like soggy cookie crumbs. Shaking from head to toe, she closed her eyes, fighting a wave of dizziness.

Safe. She laid her palm on her forehead. She was perfectly safe. And no longer alone. That was her last conscious thought as she fainted.

Logan Hunter lay perfectly still. The pain in his groin seemed to have spread throughout his entire body. When the feeling passed, he assured himself he wasn't ruined for life, and the rest of him was in working order too.

Moving cautiously, he sat up and wiped rainwater from his face. He turned his head and suspiciously eyed his unwelcome intruder, who lay unmoving, spread-eagled, and dripping wet on his plush beige carpet.

A pair of beautiful, well-shaped feminine legs and a small, delicate pair of hands with short, manicured nails were the only visible parts of her. The rest was hidden by a hideous bright yellow rain slicker. The only person he'd ever seen wear one like it had been a little boy jumping puddles in a TV commercial about canned soup. Her taste in socks wasn't much better, he thought, looking at the soggy red-violet things around her nicely shaped ankles.

"Lady," he said, using the term very lightly indeed, "you've picked a hell of a night to come calling. And I don't mind telling you, your grand entrance leaves a lot to be desired. What in God's name possessed you to go running around in this weather?"

He waited for an answer. When one didn't come, it occurred to him that she hadn't so much as twitched a muscle. He leaned over and poked her shoulder. Out cold, he thought with a sigh.

Was she drunk or hurt? Who was she? What was she doing out on a night like this? What in the hell could she possibly want with him? Since no answers to those questions were forthcoming, he got up and closed the door against the rain and wind. Crossing the room to the sound system, he lowered the volume of the music, then went back to see what he could do for his unwanted guest. By the time he reached her, he saw her shaking and heard her moan softly.

As T.S. regained consciousness, she felt a movement beside her. Dully, she became aware of a hard thigh pressing against her arm. Why couldn't she stop shaking?

Logan's brows knit together in consternation as he saw spasms rack the woman's small body. "Hey, lady, are you all right?" A strange combination of compassion and belligerence mingled in his voice. "Are you hurt? You in some kind of trouble?"

Realizing she either couldn't or wouldn't respond, he bent over her and eased back the hood of her raincoat. Her eyes flickered opened as he cradled her head between his hands.

His gaze roved over her face. Shock was the only expression he could see in her eyes. Her full lips were tinged with blue, her fine-textured skin was deathly white and cold to his touch. Trying to remember what to do for someone in shock, he

rubbed her cheeks, teasing color into the pale-
ness.

T.S. stared mutely into the ice-blue eyes that
watched her with neither pity nor malice. Some
portion of her brain registered that the man was
handsome in a granite-faced sort of way. Dark
blond hair with golden highlights was neatly
combed back from his high forehead. His strong
features held a certain sensuality. At the moment
his square jaw was visibly tensed, and his firm
mouth looked as hard as his eyes.

Another working part of her mind suddenly
wondered how she must look to him. Certainly
wet, bedraggled, and wild-eyed with reminiscent
fear.

"You're the wettest wench I've ever seen," he
said, looking her over as he continued to massage
her cheeks.

Having her thoughts confirmed about the way
she looked, she closed her eyes.

He tapped one side of her face with his fingers.
"If you faint again, I'm throwing you back out into
the rain." It was an idle threat, but a good one
since she groaned in protest. "That's better. I'm
going to help you sit up, okay?"

He eased her to a sitting position and kept her
upright by bracing her back with one arm. Even
half-drowned and in shock, she was an attractive
woman. Dry and cleaned-up, she might be a
beauty, he thought, looking her over.

A thick mass of short auburn hair clung damply
around her face, contrasting perfectly with flaw-
less ivory skin. She had high cheekbones, a straight
nose, and a dusty-rose mouth set in a daintily
pointed oval face.

Her long, dark lashes fluttered upward, then

she stared at him with exquisite cornflower-blue eyes.

Cornflower blue? He racked his brain for the reason why she suddenly seemed so familiar. Then his breath caught in his throat, and his heart leaped to attention.

Recognition struck Logan like a baseball bat across his back. He was a master at hiding his emotions though, and not so much as a blink of his eyes betrayed the effect her identity had on him.

Against his will, his hand cupped her jaw and his thumb traced her full lower lip. His gaze traveled to her hair, and his hand followed. Lifting a short, damp curl from her forehead, he spared a moment's regret for the absence of silken flame tresses that had once curled down her back.

A shadow of alarm passed through his soul, displacing the wonder of rediscovering T.S. Winslow. He wanted to plant his mouth on hers and kiss her wet socks off. He wanted to pick her up and throw her back out into the foul weather. He did neither.

"We have to get you out of this raincoat," he said, forcing himself to concentrate on what had to be done. He pried the flashlight out of her stiff fingers; then, with amazing calm, he worked the snaps free. He helped her out of the garment as though she were a small child.

"Don't move. I'm going to get a towel to dry you off." Catching her chin in his hand, he forced her to meet his gaze. "Do you understand what I'm saying?"

She nodded weakly.

Logan gathered the raincoat and flashlight. He stood, gazing down at her for a second. She had been calling his office for weeks, and he'd conjured up every excuse he could think of to avoid returning those phone calls. Then she'd come looking for him at the office that morning. Now she was here. God, what was he going to do?

She'd changed so little, he thought, shaking his head in wonder as he turned away and headed for his bedroom.

Suddenly, memories from a distant and disassociated past threatened him. Pain squeezed his chest. Over the years Logan's memory had become very selective. He was an expert at closing his mind to things and people he'd chosen to forget. And a fragile-looking girl with hair the color of flames and eyes so very blue was one of those people.

Using her flashlight, he walked through the master bedroom and into the adjoining bath. He tossed the yellow horror of a raincoat into the tub.

Feeling more shaken than he wanted to admit, he stood without moving. Thoughts whirled through his mind with the force of the wild wind outside. Why was she here? What did she want from Logan Hunter? What, if anything, did she know about him? Would she recognize him? What would he do if she did?

Logan hoped she wouldn't recognize him. The odds that she wouldn't were in his favor. Between the ages of sixteen and twenty, he'd changed a great deal. His face had filled out, he had developed the lean, well-muscled body of a man, and his height had topped out at six feet. Since then, adulthood had added further subtle changes to his face.

So what if she did see some resemblance in him

to a skinny, awkward youth she'd once known briefly? Comparisons could easily be dismissed.

He could handle the ghost from his past. He *must* handle T.S. Winslow. The best course of action was to treat her as if they'd never met, never shared a tiny one-room apartment, never shared a single moment in time.

Determined to remain calm and in control, Logan grabbed a clean towel and left the room.

T.S. wearily raised her head when she heard him return. He knelt down in front of her and covered her hair with a towel, rubbing energetically enough to make her feel as if her brains were rolling around like dice.

"T.S.," she croaked, suddenly regaining her ability to speak. "My name is T.S. Winslow."

His vigorous movements stilled, then almost immediately started again. "What does T.S. stand for?"

"Ty-Tyler Scott," she stammered through chattering teeth.

"Well, Ty-Tyler Scott, what were you doing out in the middle of a gale?" His tone was lightly spiced with pleasant sarcasm.

"I'm renting the cottage next door. The storm . . . Power went off. I didn't feel safe there."

"That house is sturdier than it looks. It's survived more storms than you have. You should have had the good sense to stay put." He removed the towel from her hair.

"It's irrational, but I'm afraid of storms." She met his stern gaze. "I didn't want to be alone."

Hearing the tremor in her voice, seeing the flash of terror in her eyes, Logan understood the extent of her fear. His heart melted a little, and the splintering sensation he felt inside told him he was no longer completely in control of his universe. Involuntarily, he raised his hand and gently rubbed his knuckles along her cheek. "It's okay. You're not alone now."

"Thank you," she whispered, giving him a weak smile.

He let his hand drop down to his lap. "No problem." It was a lie. She could cause him plenty of problems. She could destroy the life he worked so hard to build.

Keeping his voice calm and even, he said, "In case you're wondering, I'm Logan Hunter."

Her eyes widened. Color drained from her face. Her small hands came together, fingers lacing and unlacing like the frantic flutter of a bird's wings. Then she let out a soft, startled cry.

Three

T.S covered her pounding heart with her hand. *"Logan Hunter?"* she repeated hoarsely.

Was it disbelief he heard in her voice? Caused by recognition of his name, or something else? Long habit and iron will kept those anxious questions from reflecting in his face.

"The one and only." The response came lightly and with a slight upturn of the corners of his mouth.

"Ni-nice to meet you," T.S. managed to say. He'd never sell her the building now, she thought frantically. Not after the way she had practically assaulted him and dripped all over his carpet.

"Let's get you up on your feet." He took her by the elbows, raising her up.

A wave of dizziness made her head spin. Her legs buckled, and she sagged against him.

In a fluid motion he lifted her into his arms. He settled her against his chest and headed for his bedroom.

She slid her arms around his shoulders. "I'm

getting you all wet. This is so embarrassing. I'm sorry I've ruined your evening."

"Yeah, you interrupted an exciting sales report." He tried to recall the statistics he had just read in order to block out his awareness of the soft lines and curves of her body, but he couldn't remember a single one.

T.S. hazily thought how warm and solid he was. Being carried by a man was . . . was sort of romantic and carnal at the same time. Wait a minute! This was Logan Hunter, a stranger, a man she simply wanted to do business with, not someone she should be thinking such thoughts about.

Searching for something to say, she blurted out, "I thought I heard Jimi Hendrix playing 'The Star-Spangled Banner.'"

"You're in shock. Probably hallucinating," he said, not really understanding why the denial came so instantly.

Entering the dark bedroom, he walked over to the king-sized bed and set her down on it. "I'll get you something dry to put on."

"Is there a Mrs. Hunter in the house?" Why was she breathlessly hoping he was single?

"No. I'm not married and never have been." A twinge of irrational jealousy made him falter as he moved away. It hadn't occurred to him she might have a husband. Lots of married women kept their maiden names. "Is there a Mr. Winslow?" he asked casually as he rummaged through the closet for a fresh shirt and a pair of jeans.

"Just my father." Neither of them were married, she thought. How nice. She fought the desire to curl up and go to sleep on his comfortable bed.

Relief passed through Logan like a prayer. Though why her marital state should matter to him was a question he didn't want to explore. Then he heard himself ask, "Ever been married?"

"Nope."

"Why not?" he grilled, going into the bathroom to get his robe.

"Don't know." She gave in to the demands of her body and sank down on the bed. The mattress was nice and firm. The quilted coverlet felt soft and cozy against her cheek. Her gaze traveled to the window that took up most of the wall beside the bed. The drapes were open. She shuddered as she saw lightning streak through the dark.

Coming back into the room, Logan said in a crisp, businesslike tone, "You've got to get out of those wet clothes. I think you're still in shock."

He halted when he saw the outline of her slender frame curled up on his bed. A purely sexual response tightened his lower body, proof positive his encounter with her knee hadn't damaged him a bit. Drawing in a sharp breath, he dumped the terry-cloth bathrobe on the bed. "I'm putting a robe beside you. Can you change by yourself or do you need help?"

The bones in her arms and legs ached. Exhaustion swept through her again. But nothing, nothing, would induce her to risk further mortification by asking for help undressing.

"I can do it." She wasn't sure she really had the energy let to lift a finger, much less her poor feet. "Shoes," she sighed like a worn-out child.

Logan had no idea if she was talking to herself or to him. "Do you want me to untie your shoes?"

"I can do it," she repeated.

"Look, I'll just get you started, okay?"

"Okay." She felt the bed dip slightly under his weight.

He didn't remember her feet being so small, Logan thought as he removed her sneakers and stripped off her socks. "There you go." He couldn't resist stroking her trim ankle. "You can do the rest," he told her, helping her sit up.

"Thank you." T.S. waited for him to leave. He merely retreated a short distance. Hoping to salvage what remained of her tattered dignity, she said, "I would prefer to be alone now."

"Rule number one. Never leave a shock victim alone."

She sighed tiredly. Undressing was going to be difficult enough for her abused muscles. With him in the room it was going to be hell on her nerves. "Do you always observe rules?"

"Of course. A world without rules produces anarchy. Don't worry, it's too dark in here for me to watch you, if that's your concern." Pleasant sarcasm once again crept into his tone. "If it makes you feel better, I intend to change my clothes too. We'll turn our backs on each other."

Knowing *he* was going to take his clothes off didn't make her feel better. It made her feel carnal again. In her best former debutante voice she said, "Please do so. Thank you."

"Whatever you say, princess."

Her hands stilled in the act of pulling the sweatshirt up. His casual use of the pet name vaguely disturbed her for a moment. Then she shrugged off the feeling along with her damp sweatshirt, her muscles screaming as she did so.

Nerve endings she didn't know she had prickled as she heard the unmistakable sound of him taking his pants off. She wondered what his lean body looked like, if his firm tush was as cute in underwear as it was in casual twill slacks, and whether he had hairy legs or not. Pushing those thoughts aside, she decided he was right about her state of shock. It wasn't like her to feel so . . . lustful.

Her energy reserve was depleted by the time she finished removing her clothing and pulled on a terry-cloth robe. "You can turn around now."

He walked back to the bed and draped a lightweight blanket around her shoulders. "Can you stand?"

She tried. The muscles in her legs refused to cooperate, and she found herself and the blanket caught up in his arms again.

Not since her childhood had she been carried so much, she thought, resting her head on his broad shoulder. It was a stimulating experience she wouldn't have any trouble getting used to, especially if he was the one providing the stimulation.

Back in the living room he placed her on a rattan sofa and tucked the blanket securely around her. "Rest for a minute. I'll get you a drink."

"Thank you." Eyes blinking adjustment to the amber light thrown off by several kerosene lamps, she watched him walk to the kitchen opening off the great room.

She glanced around the spacious area. Rattan and wicker furniture were arranged in precise groupings. The sofas and chairs were covered in coordinating patterns of polished-cotton fabric. Behind her, a wall of glass faced the desk and ocean beyond. Everywhere she looked, she saw neutral colors—beige, white-on-white, touches of black and gold. She wondered whether the lack of clutter meant the man was a neat freak, or was simply evidence of an orderly mind and an ability to minimize distractions.

She turned her attention to the paintings, hung in precise groupings. She knew enough about artwork to recognize the artist whose work was considered valuable and good—if you liked black-and-white abstracts with clean lines, and form without emotion.

A long, curving breakfast counter with tall rattan chairs separated the great room from the kitchen. Looking at all the white modernistic space, she got the impression of a blank coloring book lying open, just waiting for someone to decide which crayon to choose first. If it were her kitchen, she would choose the brightest crayon in the box.

She loved the house itself. The decor, she hated.

Her gaze shifted to Logan. She couldn't deny the strong tug of attraction she felt. It had been a very long time since she had been more than mildly interested in any man. The timing and the man were all wrong.

She watched him moving around, opening cabinets, taking glasses out of one, a bottle out of another. Something about the way he moved produced an odd feeling of familiarity. Unable to discern why she felt that way, she dismissed the idea.

Taking a closer look at him, she estimated his age to be early to mid-thirties. He'd changed into jeans that molded nicely to his hips and thighs, and a beige knit shirt that stretched interestingly over broad shoulders and provided a perfect foil for suntanned skin.

Suddenly, the low drone of a hard, pounding rock beat claimed her attention. She listened carefully. Her brows arched upward as she recognized Jethro Tull, a popular group of the early seventies. She shook her head. Hendrix and Tull.

His taste in music matched her own, but T.S. found it inconsistent with the decor and the man himself. If asked to hazard a guess based upon his appearance, she'd have come up with easy listening, perhaps classical music. As soon as those thoughts floated through her head, she chided herself. She knew better than to make judgments based on surface information. All human beings were full of surprising contradictions.

Logan came back into the sitting area, a bottle and two brandy snifters in his hands.

What was it about the way he moved? she wondered again. He was tall, maybe a fraction or so over six feet, and built lean but muscular and solid.

He set the brandy and glasses on top of the low wicker-and-glass table in front of her.

"I rarely drink," she said.

"You will tonight." Pouring out a generous measure in each snifter, he offered one to her.

"I don't like brandy."

"Tough." He sat down on the edge of the sofa by her waist. Capturing her chin in one hand, he lifted the glass to her mouth with the other. "Drink," he ordered in a voice that matched his hard blue eyes. "A little won't kill you."

Lightheaded from his touch and determined not to show it, she parted her lips and drank. Liquid fire coursed down her throat, burning a trail all the way to her stomach. She coughed violently enough to bring tears to her eyes. His helpful slap on her back wasn't the least bit helpful, and she glared at him.

"One more sip." He slid his fingers from her chin to her cheek, caressing her skin. "The color is coming back into your face."

"I believe it. My whole body is on fire," she said, not certain if her color was due to the brandy or the fascinating movement of his hand on her cheek. Taking another small sip of the liquid, she found it a little more palatable but nonetheless abrasive. "I can't imagine why my father thinks this firewater is the only civilized drink."

Something akin to humor twitched the corners of his mouth. "I quite agree. It *is* the only civilized drink."

Picking up his own snifter, he moved to a nearby chair that faced the sofa. He lowered his long body into it and looked down at the dark liquid in his glass. "So, Ty-Tyler Scott Winslow, what do you do when you're not running around in foul weather and tackling strange men?"

"It's just Tyler."

"I know." He met her gaze.

She smiled sheepishly. "Oh, you're teasing me." It was difficult to tell when his mouth looked as if it had to work hard for a smile. Again the odd tinge of familiarity sparked her nerve endings. Shades of *déjà vu*, she thought, feeling bewildered.

"I'm on the All Saints board of directors in Greensboro," she said, answering his question.

Logan studied her thoughtfully over the rim of his brandy snifter as he remembered the young T.S. saying her father expected her to go into the family furniture business. What had happened to change that? he wondered. "I believe I recently read something about All Saints. It's a charitable organization. All board members are volunteers, aren't they?"

"That's correct."

"Are you employed elsewhere?"

"No. All Saints takes up the majority of my time

and energy. My official capacity is head of finances, so I do a great deal of fund-raising." She smiled sleepily. "That means I'm chief beggar, borrower, and thief."

"I see."

His failure to respond to her humor and his two-word commentary sounded like disapproval and censure to her. Ordinarily, she never allowed anyone else's opinion of her to matter more than her own. She could even handle her father's disapproval of how she chose to live her life. But for some reason she found herself caring about Logan's opinion and feeling defensive because she cared.

"All Saints is a worthwhile organization, Mr. Hunter," she said with a slight chill in her voice. "We operate and support a wide variety of services and programs for the homeless—a soup kitchen, temporary shelter, free medical care, legal assistance, and personal counseling."

"We've wrestled on the floor and changed clothes together." Amusement wove through his words like colored ribbons. "Under the circumstances, I think you should call me Logan. And by the way, I wasn't being critical."

"I thought you were. Forgive me. I guess I'm feeling a little oversensitive."

"After what you've been through tonight, that's understandable. Are you here for business or pleasure?"

She sipped her brandy and hugged the blanket a little closer. "I'm surprised you don't recognize my name."

Wariness flickered in his eyes; then they steadied into a bland expression. "Why are you surprised?"

"I've phoned your office no less than a dozen times in the past few weeks. You don't look like a man who would tolerate inefficient employees. Therefore, I assume you received my messages."

He stretched his legs out as though getting into a comfortable position for a cozy chat with a friend. "Why did you wish to contact me?"

Annoyed by his refusal either to confirm or deny receiving her messages, T.S. started to take another drink but found her glass empty. "I want to buy the apartment building you recently acquired in Greensboro." She leaned over to the table to pick up the bottle and poured another measure of brandy into her snifter.

He rested his chin on his fist, giving her a speculative look. "For what purpose? How do you propose to finance it?" Then he added bluntly, "You're unemployed."

"Run a credit check on me." She smiled. "I want to turn it into a shelter for runaway kids."

Logan's brows rose as he wondered how much of her interest in runaways stemmed from her own experience. Deciding to go on the offensive, he drawled, "Runaway kids. The homeless. Quite the humanitarian, aren't you? Or are you a little rich girl who hasn't decided what to do with her life yet?" Immediately, he felt like a jerk for baiting her, but he wanted to know if the adult T.S. was made of sterner stuff than the youthful one.

Fixing him with an unblinking stare, she shot up to a sitting position. "Making money isn't the only worthy objective in life, Mr. Hunter." She clutched the back of the sofa with one hand and braced the snifter against her chest with the other, waiting for a wave of dizziness to subside before continuing. "I'm very serious about what I do."

He was silent for a moment. "Yes, I can see that you are."

"I'm sure you don't know this, but the rat fink who sold that piece of property to you did so knowing it was his late aunt's intention to donate it to All Saints. Morally, you have no right to it."

"Moral indignation is envy with a halo," he countered. "It was his right to sell it and mine to buy it."

She nodded. "That's true. I think it stinks, but it's true."

Her eyes were growing strained from the diffused, flickering light. She had to make a concentrated effort to hold his gaze. "Logan, there are so many people out there who have no choice but to live on the street. And the children . . . My God, you don't know what heartbreak is until you've seen them and talked with them. They need help. Somebody has to care."

Her head began to feel heavy. She slowly lay down again. "So, will you sell me the property?"

"It isn't for sale. I have plans for it."

T.S. vaguely realized it wouldn't do any good to push the issue further. Besides, she wasn't in fighting form at the moment. She changed the subject, choosing the first thing that came to mind. "Logan, this room is too vanilla."

"It is not. It was professionally decorated." He sounded a trifle annoyed.

"Well, then that explains it." She kicked off the blanket. "It's awfully warm in here, isn't it?"

"What does it explain?" he asked.

She raised her hand, gesturing lazily. "No color. Too bland. I just have a feeling it really doesn't reflect your personality."

When he didn't answer, she turned her head to look at him. Something in his expression revealed that her observation had thrown him off balance.

"At least your taste in music isn't vanilla," she went on. "Do you know what I wish? I wish I had been older in the late sixties and early seventies. I was too young to get involved with what was happening then."

Again, surprise flashed in his eyes but was quickly concealed. T.S. knew she'd somehow thrown him another curveball. She tried to figure out why, but it was too difficult to think clearly. Obviously, brandy and exhaustion were a lethal combination.

"It was a weird time," he said offhandedly.

"Wrong, it was a great time. People didn't just talk about what they believed in. They had dreams and ideals. They believed they could change the world and tried to. I admire them for that."

"They were idealistic fools who finally grew up to become stock brokers, lawyers, doctors, and politicians."

She grinned at his cynical attitude. "And we went on to become a kinder, gentler nation."

"Are you a hopeless idealist, T.S.?"

"No. I'm full of hope."

Falling silent, she dully became aware of the wind rushing past the house in ferocious bursts. How odd, she thought just before her eyelids fluttered closed. For a while she'd forgotten about the storm.

A few minutes later Logan realized she'd drifted off to sleep. The muscles in his face relaxed.

She looked utterly charming and innocently sensual in her current state of dishabille. His gaze roved over her, picking out details—skin kissed pink from the sun; the rich, flame-colored hair in thick, rapidly curling disorder; the beautiful flush spreading across her cheeks; the finely arched brows. His robe had slipped down one shoulder, revealing the curving slope of her breasts. One shapely leg was bent and resting against the sofa pillow.

He raised his brandy glass, fighting the image of a slender girl wearing a tie-dyed shirt as she sat kicking her heels and looking at him with hero worship in her eyes. That image dissolved into another of those same deep blue eyes brimming with hurt and betrayal.

Guilt, all-encompassing, as threatening as the turbulent ocean waves, as fresh and raw as the day it was born sixteen years ago, swiftly filled his conscience. He'd deceived her then for her own good. Now it was for his own survival.

He'd rewritten his life, made himself over so thoroughly, even he believed it. His past was buried so deeply inside him, it was more fantasy than reality.

Since the first message he'd received from her, he'd had a feeling of impending disaster. Two worlds colliding with an explosive impact. He had hoped to avoid it. He *would* avoid it.

He got up and walked over to her. Gazing down at her, he breathed in the scent of her unusual perfume. She even smelled the same. Like spring flowers and spices.

He closed his eyes, allowing the fragrance to take him back to another place, another time. He fleetingly remembered her telling him the perfume had been a gift from her mother—the last she was ever to receive. It had been blended specially for her by a parfumeur in New Orleans.

For a moment Logan could swear he heard the blood singing through his veins, drowning out the sounds of the storm. He shook his head, finding it difficult to believe that after all the years gone by, she still possessed the ability to wring emotions out of his heart of stone.

With an odd pang of regret he forced the small memory back where it belonged. When it was safely locked away, he bent down, taking the empty glass from her fine-boned hand that was barely larger than a child's.

Her eyes opened, staring up at him. "I'm not giving up," she murmured, then drifted off to sleep again.

"That's what I'm afraid of," he said softly.

He was very much afraid that the lovely girl he'd rescued in a bus station had slipped back into his carefully constructed life.

In his mind a warning signal went off like a flare shot up into a moonless night sky. Without knowing it, T.S. Winslow had already scratched off a thin layer of his veneer.

T.S. woke early the next morning, startled out of a distorted dream by the quietness. With the sense of something not being quite right, she struggled to sit up.

Her gaze swept around a room she didn't recognize, taking in the brass headboard of the bed she couldn't remember getting into. Splendid yellow light filled the small bedchamber, seeming to ricochet off every sea-foam-green and white surface and stabbing at her sensitive eyes.

The wind had quit, she suddenly noticed. All was quiet except for the sound of running water coming from somewhere above her.

"Logan Hunter," she groaned as the events of the previous evening rushed back to her. Apparently, she'd passed out on his sofa and he'd put her to bed.

Fleetingly, she regretted not being aware of the pleasant sensation of him holding her, carrying her around as if she were as light as a child.

Then she remembered what an absolute fool she had made of herself. If he thought her sanity quota was a quart low, she wouldn't blame him a bit. Lord, she had even kneed him in the groin, something a man wasn't likely to forget in a hurry.

She lowered her head, which felt stuffed with cotton, into her hands. A little fresh air might help, she decided. Throwing back the bed linens, she got up. The white robe she was wearing was twisted around her body, so she rearranged it and tightened the belt.

Feeling a little unsteady, she walked out to the wide corridor. Through an open doorway to her left, she saw a neatly organized office. The decor was ultra modern and expensive. She sighed over the black-and-white color scheme.

A quick survey of the other rooms revealed a tan-and-beige bedroom and a small sitting room only slightly more colorful in shades of alabaster, smoky gray, and pale peach. Deciding Logan's decorator had been a color minimalist to the max, she climbed the steps of a curving, freestanding staircase.

It led to a hallway. She passed a closed door. The master bedroom? The hall opened up into the great room she remembered from the night before.

She saw the deck beyond a wall of glass, and went outside.

The breeze, light and slightly cool, felt good upon her face. She looked up at the cloudless sky, then down past the eelgrass swaying on top of the dunes. A line of foam lay where the water had lapped up the side. She shivered to think how close it had come.

Glancing around, she saw she had a choice of sitting in one of two wet rocking chairs or on a built-in bench at the far end of the deck. She chose the bench.

Leaning back, she turned her gaze to the beach. The sand bubbled with ghostly white mole crabs. Black-headed gulls poked at the sand, searching for small crustaceans. She noticed how the sun tickled the waves with ribbons of light. The surf was amazingly calm. Frothy foam festooned the shore. Spray from the surf had turned the air milky and thick.

Everything moved. The breakers. Seabound froth. Even the stranded foam in shimmering colors of pink, purple, and blue.

Peacefulness only heightened the numb sensation produced by the night's fear, too much brandy, and a fitful slumber filled with disturbing images.

Why had she dreamed of Moon Man last night? she wondered, an ache suddenly tightening her throat. It had been years since he had invaded the privacy of her sleep. She wasn't happy with the way the memory of her first love could still trigger a pocket of anguish trapped inside her.

T.S. closed her eyes. Her head throbbed as she recalled the confusing dream.

She'd been lost in the storm on the beach, running from the black surf. Someone was running ahead of her. Moon Man. She called his name. He stopped and turned slowly. Elated to find him, she held out her hands as she rushed toward him. He began to shimmer like phosphorescence in the cresting waves, then he was gone. Falling to her knees in despair, she wept. Gentle hands, Logan's hands, lifted her. As she gazed up into his face, he, too, began to shimmer and fade.

She shook her head, wondering what to make of that confusing dream. Putting her feet on the bench, she hugged her legs and dropped her chin to rest on her knees. She breathed in the crisp ocean air and tried to focus her mind on nothing more strenuous than the ebb and flow of the morning tide, but her mind refused to cooperate.

She sighed wearily. Would she ever be completely free of the chains that boy had wrapped around her heart?

Four

Logan went downstairs to the guest room. He stopped outside the door and took a deep breath. One last look was all he would allow himself before he firmly ejected her from his house and his life. Squaring his shoulders, he walked in slowly. He came out fast.

She wasn't there. Strange, disquieting thoughts filled his head as he searched through every room on the first floor. She was really gone.

He ascended the stairs to the second level, feeling bewildered and a little angry at his reaction.

Upstairs, he walked to the window and gazed out at the ocean. Then he saw her. She sat at the far end of the deck, looking like a calm port after a stormy voyage.

Relief played chase with the other emotions hovering unwanted in his chest. He was *not* glad she was still there, he told himself, turning away.

T.S. Winslow didn't mean a thing to him, he thought as he marched into the kitchen. He opened a cabinet and grabbed two mugs. She was nothing but trouble. He slammed the cabinet shut. The sooner she left, the better. He poured coffee into both mugs.

Whirling on his heel, he abruptly found himself facing a pile of feminine clothing on the breakfast bar. It made a brilliant splash of color on the white tiles. He grimaced and headed for the deck.

"Good morning," he said as he walked outside.

She looked up and smiled brightly. "It's amazingly beautiful this morning. So calm and peaceful."

For a moment he was riveted where he stood. "Yes, it always is after a storm," he said politely as his heated gaze traveled over her hair. He noticed the way it gleamed in the sunlight, and he wanted to touch the curls the breeze stirred at her nape. He took a deep breath and moved toward her.

T.S. felt the power of his gaze, a power intensified by the flicker of frank masculine interest in his eyes. She only had a second to register the fleeting emotion before it was replaced by something more aloof.

"I made coffee." He handed her one of the mugs he held. "It's black. I didn't know how you like it."

"Black is fine. Thank you." She watched him abruptly turn to face the sea.

Logan felt tension seeping into his muscles. He didn't want to think about how right she looked wearing his robe. Nor did he want the sudden memory of a younger girl dressed in a borrowed tie-dyed shirt. It only opened old wounds and reminded him of the price he paid for being someone else.

The way to handle the situation had seemed so clear to him when he couldn't sleep last night. Give her coffee in the morning. Make her understand the property wasn't for sale. Send her home. Get her out of his life as soon as possible.

His resolve had weakened the moment he had gone downstairs and not found her. The flood of emotions he'd experienced confirmed he wanted her. Wise or not, he wanted the grown up T.S. Winslow as much if not more than he had wanted the girl.

Don't be an idiot, he told himself, giving his survival instinct a mental shove. Further involvement with her meant risking the life he knew. He had everything he ever dreamed of having. She was a threat to be neutralized. He would follow his plan of action, no matter how tempting she might be.

"Do you always dress so formally on Saturday mornings, or are you going to work?" she asked, breaking into his thoughts.

"I'm leaving for the office in a few minutes."

T.S. heard the coolness in his voice. He looked every inch the successful businessman in his conservatively tailored navy suit trousers, crisp white shirt, and red striped tie. "Apparently, you haven't embraced the latest American trend. Fast-track careers are out. Cocooning is in. The Me Decade is gone. Getting involved on the community level is in."

"Sounds like nineties pop jargon," he said, looking faintly amused. "Involvement and cocooning are contradictory terms."

She laughed softly. "Not necessarily. One can do both. It means rejecting the rat race, getting off the fast track. Choosing to spend more time at home with family and friends. Enjoying the simple things." She lifted her mug and saluted him. "Like sharing a cup of coffee with someone and watching the day begin."

Logan thought about that for a moment, letting his gaze whisper over the richly colored hair clustered in short curls around her delicate face. In his own way, he realized, he had cocooning down to a fine art. But his cocoon held only himself.

Frowning, he glanced away. "I don't have a family," he said brusquely. Why did saying those words produce an emptiness inside him?

T.S. stretched her legs out and crossed one ankle over the other. Did he ever cut loose and truly indulge in a lengthy conversation? she wondered. What a complicated, moody man he was. Her gaze shifted to his profile.

Last night, she'd thought him attractive. Lamplight softens, though. By daylight his features were more sharply defined, more powerful, more unyielding, though not a bit less attractive. Sunlight revealed his force of character—harder, leaner, more intense. This morning, his ice-blue eyes seemed so distant.

Unexpectedly, another flash of elemental recognition idled through her subconscious like a sleepwalker. She struggled to understand the myriad impressions racing through her mind. Then she knew. Logan Hunter reminded her of Moon Man! More than likely, that was why she'd had that strange dream the night before.

There were some striking similarities between them, she mused, gazing at him thoughtfully. The square jaw, the hard eyes, and the gentle touch. Like Moon Man, Logan outwardly displayed No Trespassing signs, but she sensed something warmer, more vulnerable, inside.

Uneasy with her own thoughts, she shifted her gaze back to the ocean. It crossed her mind that one of the reasons she was attracted to Logan was because of that resemblance to Moon Man.

"So," he said, "I suppose you'll be leaving today?"

She blinked slowly and looked up at him again. His attitude was one of quiet watchfulness. The tone of his voice had been pleasant enough, but she detected an unspoken *I hope* attached to his inquiry.

Her curiosity soared. Last night he'd asked all the questions, revealing little about himself. Then as now, she was certain she had seen quickly subdued glimpses of sensual interest in his severe eyes. She puzzled over the mixed signals he gave off. When he wasn't hiding his feelings, his eyes told her to stay. His words, though, told her to get lost and good riddance.

"No, I think I'll be around for a while." For reasons she couldn't explain to herself, she wanted to get to know this intriguingly mysterious man. And it had nothing to do with his resemblance to a boy who had passed so briefly through her life, she told herself.

"You're wasting your time," he said. "The property isn't for sale."

The frigid certainty in his voice puzzled her, as did the feeling that a truckload of tension had just been dumped onto the deck. "Why not?"

"I have plans for it."

She sighed. "You don't give much information away, do you? What kind of plans?"

He didn't respond to that. The warning gleam in his eyes made it clear he didn't intend to discuss the matter any further. She resisted the impulse to push and canceled her plan to stage a sit-in at Hunter Properties.

His reticence to sell didn't bother her. In her fund-raising ventures she'd handled more difficult cases than Logan Hunter. Opening knotted purse strings was something she did rather well. It merely took time and patience. She had plenty of both.

She stood, turning to face him. "I don't believe I thanked you for last night. I appreciate your taking me in and being so kind."

Logan couldn't look away from her smile. It reflected such warmth and sincerity. "I wasn't being kind," he said, slowly and very plainly. "I am not a kind man."

She shook her head. "You could have thrown me back out into the storm. But you didn't. You gave me dry clothes, shelter, and comfort."

He met her gaze. Her eyes, he suddenly discovered, no longer held the essence of tragedy that had once tugged on his heart. He saw in them now a confidence and intelligence, and an almost childlike sense of being at peace with herself.

But even as an adult, wrapped in a robe too large for her slender frame and her hair wildly tangled in disordered curls, she still looked like a princess to him. And she was as unavailable to him now as she had been then.

Mixed feelings fought within him. For one long minute he felt as though he stood on the edge of the Grand Canyon. His slightest wrong movement could send him toppling helplessly over the edge.

Common sense and self-preservation told him to put as much distance between them as possible. But desire, he was discovering, was a strange, willful emotion. It generated its own force. Compelling. Dynamic. Immune to common sense.

The desire he'd felt for the young girl was nothing compared to what he felt for the woman she'd become. Without realizing his intention, he reached out to lift her chin and brought his mouth down roughly on hers.

Her lips parted under the onslaught. Instinctively, she raised her hand to clasp his shoulder.

T.S. found kissing Logan disconcertingly intense. Just like the man himself. All heat and power. Solid and strong.

He broke away and stepped back. "I'm sorry. I shouldn't have done that," he said, his expression remote, his tone deceptively polite.

She gazed at him, her eyes soft and bemused. "No apology necessary. I liked it."

As candid as ever, he thought. T.S. hadn't lost her tendency to naively say whatever she was feeling.

Yet he sensed the woman possessed strengths the girl had not. Charming and dangerous.

For a man who prided himself on total control over his emotions, he realized he rapidly lost that control whenever she was near. Get a grip, he told himself.

He infused stiffness into his backbone. He even managed an urbane smile. "I left your clothes on the breakfast bar. Lock the door when you leave. Have a good trip back to Greensboro."

T.S. said nothing at all. She studied the determined set of his shoulders as he stalked into the house and out of sight.

Taking a deep breath, she faced the ocean. The coffee mug trembled faintly in her hand. She was more shaken by what had just occurred than she'd realized. Shaken by his intensity. Shaken because she had never been more keenly aware, both physically and emotionally, of another person.

"T.S., you just screwed up big time," she chided herself. Her interest in Logan Hunter had just moved out of the business category and into the personal. Very personal.

Not wise, she thought. The man was an unapproachable wall of fire. Anyone who attempted to walk through the flames would get burned. Maybe she was a little crazy, but she felt compelled to try.

Her necklace was missing. T.S. frantically tore through the bedroom in her rented cottage, scattering clothes right and left, letting them lie where they fell.

"Oh please," she whispered, dropping down on her knees and hands to look under the bed. "Please, be here." It wasn't under the bed or the dresser. She crawled around, searching every square inch of the floor.

Slowly, she got up and sat on the bed. Her head bowed; her body slumped. She closed her eyes, fighting the intense desolation sweeping over her.

T.S. would never forget the first time she saw the medallion lying against Moon Man's smooth chest. *Love endures like the moon and the stars.* She swallowed hard, remembering his response to her curious questions about the medallion and what it meant. His eyes had taken on a sad, haunted look when she'd asked him who had given him the necklace.

She could still remember how furiously her heart had beat when he'd given the necklace to her, and how warm it had felt from lying against his body. Sunlight had sparkled on the crescent moon and stars, making them come alive.

I'll wear it always.

And she had, she raged silently. She had worn it every day for sixteen years. The only time it left her body was when she bathed, and on rare occasions when more formal jewelry was required. It had become so much a part of her, she felt naked and bereft without it.

How could she not have noticed it was gone? "Think," she told herself. She knew she had been wearing it when she had run out into the storm. It could have come off when she removed her sweatshirt in Logan's bedroom last night. It was the only place it could be, the only place she hadn't searched, couldn't search until he came home.

"Please be there," she whispered again.

Logan was not in a good mood when he returned home after ten o'clock that evening. It didn't improve his disposition a bit when he saw the brightly lit little cottage next door.

T.S. was still there. Just knowing she was close by sent anger and a hot flood of desire shooting through him. He realized he wasn't certain what to do with those feelings any more than he knew what to do about her.

That faint twinge of uncertainty followed him up the deck stairs. Nothing had gone right since the wind blew T.S. into his stomach last night, he thought irritably.

Even his dinner date with Melissa had gone haywire. *Especially* his date with her. He couldn't put his finger on why he hadn't enjoyed the evening or what exactly had gone wrong. All through the meal, though, he'd experienced a growing uneasiness. Something was missing. *What?*

Melissa didn't have the earthiness of a flower child or the fragile beauty of someone like T.S. Melissa wasn't the domestic type. He didn't expect her to be. His dream of a house with a white picket fence and a Donna Reed clone in the kitchen had long fallen by the wayside. It hadn't been a realistic dream to begin with.

She was an excellent businesswoman. In the six months Melissa had been with Hunter Properties, she'd sold over 83 million worth of real estate. She was attractive, well-dressed, a pleasant companion, and like himself only interested in the present and future. Melissa never made emotional waves.

He'd taken her out occasionally over the last few months, and he'd been thinking of becoming more seriously involved with her. Until that evening, he'd considered Melissa the perfect wife for someone like himself. But looking at her across the restaurant table, he suddenly couldn't imagine spending the rest of his life with her.

At the top of the deck he turned again to look down at T.S.'s cottage. A cold prickle of awareness crawled up the back of his neck as he felt the temptation to repeat his foolish mistake in kissing her. In the end he resisted, summoning the self-discipline he needed to put the key in the lock of his door.

Once he was inside, his discipline faltered. The main room felt cold, empty, and dark. It was as though T.S. had taken all the life out of it when she left.

He switched on the overhead light. Glancing around the room as if for the first time, he took in the white-on-white and shades of beige decor. Neutral, bland, uninteresting. Vanilla, she'd called it.

It was what he'd wanted and worked for, he thought as he stalked out of the room and down the hall. A vanilla life. To be the same as everybody else.

Damn T.S. for seeing through the things he'd surrounded himself with. For making him feel different. He'd been accepted at face value for so long, he'd forgotten what it was like to feel that way.

In his bedroom he turned on a lamp, stripped off his suit jacket, and flung it onto a chair. Sitting on the bed, he bent over to untie his shoes.

A bit of silver, partially hidden by the bedspread, winked up at him from the ecru carpet. He reached for it. Apparently, it was a necklace that had fallen out of the atrocious green sweatshirt he'd picked up off the floor that morning.

He sat up slowly, holding on to the long, thin silver chain. His gaze locked on the medallion dangling from the end of the necklace. Shock kept him perfectly still.

A voice from the past, his father's mellow baritone, whispered from the dark recesses of his memory. *Love endures as surely as the moon and stars shine bright in the liquid light of heaven. May you never lose your way. Happy birthday, son.*

Logan's shoulders heaved as he dragged air into his lungs. The medallion had been given to him on his tenth birthday. He in turn had given it to T.S.

Just moments before he betrayed her.

Love endures. She still wore the necklace. After all these years, could a spark of feeling remain inside her for that boy? What could it possibly mean to her?

Elbows resting on his thighs, he let the necklace sift from one hand to the other. In the short time since T.S. had come back into his life, she'd taught him a couple of lessons. The past wasn't as dead as he wanted to believe, and not everything was within his control. He didn't particularly appreciate either lesson.

A suffocating sensation tightened his throat. The room began to close in on him. Out. He had to get out where he could breathe.

He slipped the chain over his head. Impatiently,

he pulled off his shoes, then stripped off all his clothing except for his briefs and his shirt, which he left unbuttoned and hanging open. In the closet he found jeans and running shoes to put on.

Minutes later, he left the house and bolted down the stairs. He headed for a dimly lit wooden walkway to the beach.

The night sky was cloudless and lit by a nearly full moon. The breeze was light and from the southwest. Logan drew in deep breaths of the pleasantly warm air. The sound of the surf and the smell of saltwater soothed him.

From the top of the walkway steps he saw a pale female form sitting at the bottom. He knew it was T.S. Quietly, he descended toward her.

"Logan, is that you?" she called out softly.

"Yes." The fragrance of her unusual perfume drifted up to meet him as he came to stand in front of her. The scent of spring flowers and spices invoked a long-forgotten memory.

"There's songs to be sung, dreams to be dreamed, and wildflowers to be picked today, Moon Man my love!"

The sweet voice of Summer Chase drifted up from the recesses of Logan's mind. He could see his mother's image so clearly. Sunlight formed a shining corona around her white-blond hair. Her long handmade skirt swirled around her ankles as she swung her five-year-old son in a circle. She kissed his cheek, then set him down. Together they would take the fine strong baskets the Rainbow Woman made and fill them with wildflowers. They would dry them and later add sweet-smelling spices. During the long winter the scent would fill every room of the communal living quarters as a reminder that after the snow was gone, spring would come again to their mountain home.

Logan shook his head, trying to clear his mind of things he didn't want to remember. "What are you doing out this time of night?" he asked.

"I'm locked out," she said sheepishly, hugging her primrose cotton dress around her knees and digging her bare toes into the soft sand. "I decided to go for a walk and forgot the key to the cottage. The door locked behind me. Are you any good at breaking and entering?"

He stared down at her. She looked so beautiful in the pale stream of moonlight. That morning he had convinced himself she meant nothing to him. Now he absorbed a welter of sensations—physical, mental, emotional. He drank in the feel of her presence, letting pleasure at the sight of her override uncertainties and good sense.

Something close to a smile, and yet more intimate than one, settled upon his lips. "This is getting to be habit, T.S. Winslow. I'm beginning to think it's my lot in life to continually rescue you from one situation or another."

He leaned forward, bracing himself with a hand on each of the wooden handrails. If he bent down, he could press his mouth to the top of her head. That thought was followed by a bewildering tangle of emotions.

"Twice isn't a habit," she said, sounding a bit ruffled. "And getting locked out could happen to anyone."

Three times, he silently responded. Aloud, he said, "With you it is. Tell me, who takes care of you when I'm not around?"

"Logan Hunter, are you asking me if there's a

special man in my life?" The effort to keep amusement out of her voice failed.

With a start of surprise, he realized that was exactly what he wanted to know. Then again, if the answer was yes, he knew he wouldn't like it at all. "Is there?" he asked calmly.

"Just one at the moment . . . my father."

"No lover?"

"No. So can you?"

His heart skipped a beat. Could he be her lover? From somewhere in his head came a resounding "absolutely." "Yes," he said, wondering if he'd lost his mind.

"Good. I was afraid I'd have to spend the night on the beach."

"Oh right, you're locked out." Did he sound as bewildered as he felt? he wondered. "I'll take a look at the lock. If it's the kind I think it is, it can be sprung with a credit card. I was just going for a walk. Would you like to come along?" It astonished him how much he wanted her to be with him. Just for a little while, he told himself.

"I would like that very much." T.S. smiled up at him. All through the day, her thoughts hadn't strayed far from Logan Hunter and her lost necklace. Just minutes before he'd arrived, she'd been working up her nerve to knock on his door, uncertain of the reception she'd receive.

She accepted the hand he held out to her. When she was standing, he didn't relinquish possession of her hand or step back. She found herself close to the warmth of his body. Vitally aware of him, she shivered.

"You're trembling. Are you cold?"

"No. I think it's just my reaction to you."

"Do I make you nervous?" He had a feeling he was about to be pushed off balance again.

"Not at all," she answered honestly. "It's strange, really, but I feel very comfortable with you. You're familiar to me somehow. I mean, I know I don't know you, but I'd like to."

T.S. absorbed his silence, realizing she'd made him uneasy. "Maybe we knew each other in a past life," she suggested jokingly. "Do you believe in reincarnation?"

"No." Her coming so close to the truth lent vehemence to the single word.

With a gentle tug on her hand, he strolled toward the surf. Awareness of the woman walking beside him howled through his consciousness like a tornado and kept him locked in his own thoughts.

They left the soft, dry sand behind to tread along the hard, wet surface left by the incoming waves. T.S. pulled away to move closer to the water, occasionally letting the cool saltwater nibble at her toes.

When she could no longer stand the silence, or ignore the growing need to take a tentative step into his wall of fire, she thought of the most outrageous—and most intimate—question one stranger could ask another. "Do you like your life, Logan?"

"I beg your pardon?" came his startled reply.

She allowed herself a quick grin. "When we're young, we all have visions of what our lives will be like when we're adults. Mine isn't at all what I envisioned, but I'm happy with the way things turned out. What about you?"

He stopped walking and stared at her in the moonlight. She was conscious of him carefully selecting his words before he spoke. It was as if she'd offered him a can of worms and he was trying to decide if he wanted to open it or not.

"It's exactly what I intended it to be," he said, then added firmly, "I like my life. How is yours different from what you imagined?"

T.S. fingered the ends of the multicolored scarf she'd tied around her waist for a belt as she considered the way Logan had swiftly bounced the conversational ball back into her court. She'd hoped for more from him. But she was also wise enough to know that sometimes one had to open up and give a little to get something in return.

"Winslow Furniture Company has been the family business for generations," she said. "My father had hoped for a son who would someday take it over. But there was just me. The last Winslow in the bunch. I grew up knowing what was expected of me, and I simply accepted it as the way things would be. Until I was sixteen, it never occurred to me that I had a voice in deciding what I would do with my life."

"I've heard of Winslow Furniture," he said. "It's a multimillion-dollar business. I would think it would be exciting to be a part of it."

"It isn't. At least, not for me. I did try, though, for my father." She started to walk again, and he moved with her. "I went away to college and earned a business degree to please him. Then I worked with him for a year. It was a miserable time for both of us. After that, I went to work full time for All Saints and never regretted it."

She glanced up at him. "Where did you grow up?"

"Norfolk, Virginia." The answer didn't come as easily to him as it usually did, for he could feel the medallion lying against his skin. He knew he'd have to give it back to her, but he was reluctant to do so. It wouldn't hurt to hold on to it a little longer.

"Tell me about yourself," said T.S., trying to dig

deeper. "I want to know everything. Who are you? Where did you go to college? Have you ever been married? Are you involved with anyone? Do you ever take a day off?"

"You don't give up, do you?" His tone barely concealed his irritation.

"Nope," she answered cheerfully. "I'd be a lousy fund-raiser if I did. You might as well sing like a canary and get it over with."

Grudgingly, he gave her high marks for her persistence. He might as well feed her his brief history and hope it was enough to appease her curiosity. "I'm the son of a career navy man and a kindergarten teacher. They died not long after I graduated from high school. I joined the navy, and then earned a degree from Virginia Tech." His voice became more terse as he spoke. The medallion seemed to grow heavier. "I was with a real estate company in Virginia Beach for a couple of years. Then I moved here and started my own business. I've never been married. I'm not involved. And no, I don't take much time off. Satisfied?"

"Not even close. That's superficial stuff," she shot back disdainfully. "It's the kind of information you read on a résumé. Paltry. You can do better than that."

Why couldn't she accept what he chose to tell her? he wondered. Everyone else did. He reached out to touch her hair where it curled seductively at her nape. "I've told you who I am. That's all you need to know."

T.S. stifled a small sigh of pleasure as his fingers skimmed lightly over her skin. "You don't make it easy for anyone to really get to know you, do you?" she murmured. Then she ventured, "Parents always have a plan for their children. Did your father want you to be a career navy man like him?"

Her probing was becoming difficult for him to handle. He curved his hand around her neck, drawing her closer. "I don't want to discuss the past. It doesn't interest me, It's the present and future that count."

"But it's the past that makes us who we are today."

"Ty-Tyler Scott, you talk too much. Ask too many questions." He whispered a kiss across her lips as he spoke.

T.S. was vividly aware of him standing so close, brushing his mouth over hers, touching her with one hand. She wanted to lessen the small space between them, but before she could follow through, he lifted his head.

"If you want to talk about the past," he said, "tell me about yours. How did a princess like you get into working with the homeless and runaway teenagers?"

A strange tension gripped her. She stepped back from him. The surf caressed her ankles and rolled away again.

"T.S.?" He spoke her name hesitantly. "Is something wrong?"

Her hand came up to cover her heart, as though in doing so she could calm its pounding. "You called me princess," she whispered. "I remember you called me that last night too."

"If it distresses you, I won't say it again." He knew he'd made a mistake, but he wasn't certain what it was. "I didn't mean it as an insult."

"I . . . I didn't take it as one. It's just—" She turned to face the ocean. Another wave came in stronger than the last. She felt it pool around the hem of her long dress. "Someone else used to call me princess. I guess it startles me to hear you use that pet name because you remind me so much of him."

A small burst of panic flared to life in the pit of Logan's stomach. He quickly squelched it. "Who was it? An old boyfriend?"

T.S. took a deep breath. Running her hand through her hair, she slowly turned to face him. "Not exactly. But he was important to me. We were just kids, and we were only together for a week. I—I loved him. That boy . . ."

She fell silent as she thought of the medallion. Pain touched her heart. In a voice full of emotion she whispered, "Moon Man changed the course of my life."

The shock that ripped through Logan's body was severe. The warm breeze licked at the cold sweat beads that formed on his palms and forehead. Time moved heavily, the seconds rising and collapsing like the ocean waves.

When his senses finally woke again, it was all he could do to say hoarsely, "How did he change you?"

Five

T.S. sensed his tension. She knew her display of emotions and frankness made him uncomfortable. "This conversation is too heavy for strangers. We've just met. I won't be offended if you would rather not hear the intimate details of my life," she said, offering him a tactful way out.

"Please go on." He placed his hand on her shoulder, communicating his willingness to listen.

"Are you—" Her thoughts scattered to the wind as his hand drifted lightly over her shoulder. She swallowed hard when his thumb traced the rapidly pulsating artery in her throat. She started over again. "Are you sure I won't bore you?"

"Not at all. T.S., I doubt you could be boring if you tried."

She closed her eyes for a moment, savoring the sensation of his palm traveling in a slow circle over her shoulder blade. The warmth of his skin penetrated through her clothing like soothing balm. Then he withdrew his hand, leaving her oddly bereft.

"You do remind me of Moon Man," she said, her voice coming out as a sigh. "I guess it's your eyes and the shape of your face. His hair was lighter than yours. More like sunlight on golden wheat. Moon Man saved my life, but I don't think he really wanted to. You took me in last night and gave me comfort, but I don't think you wanted to either."

She paused briefly, giving him a chance to respond. He remained silent, so she continued. "I ran away from home when I was sixteen. Ended up in a bus station in Richmond, Virginia, where a pimp tried to pick me up. I was so dumb, I didn't even know what he was until Moon Man rescued me and later explained the situation. How's that for being naive?"

Logan answered slowly, "Someone who has been sheltered and protected all his life doesn't expect the world to be a cruel place."

His own first clashes with the world outside the commune came back to him in kaleidoscope images. Holding tight to his father's hand as a peace march erupted in violence. Taunts and jeers delivered with the childish cruelty of other six-year-olds in a rural school yard.

He mentally shook his head. He felt as if he were standing on the fine line between reality and illusion.

"Moon Man and I spent a week together in the roughest section of the city," T.S. went on. "He fed me and kept me safe." Emotion swelled in her chest. "He called me an ivory-tower princess, but he was the only person besides my mother who didn't treat me like one. When I talked, he listened. One night he held me and let me cry in grief over my mother's death. He didn't offer false comfort, or tell me not to cry, or say any of the pointless things people tend to say. I wish I could tell him what a healing gift he gave me."

A wave crested over her bare feet, again soaking the hem of her dress. Millions of grains of sand shifted beneath her as the water receded. "Moon Man and my experience with him helped me understand how sheltered my life had been. I guess you could say I suddenly woke up and saw things I never knew existed—poverty, hunger, the kind of despair and desperation that drives human beings to abuse themselves and others. I'd never had to fight to survive like the people we encountered. When I went back to the luxury of my own life, I wasn't the same person. I couldn't go back to being an ivory-tower princess with a Marie Antoinette let-them-eat-cake attitude."

Logan's head spun with all she'd told him. When he'd set out to change his own life, it hadn't occurred to him his actions would spread like tentacles, touching everyone in his path. He'd considered no one but himself. How arrogantly naive, he thought bitterly.

Rescuing T.S. had been a good thing. But keeping her with him had changed how she looked at the world and her future. In turn, it had even changed her father's life, robbing him of an heir to a business that had been in their family for generations.

And what of his own parents? Logan allowed himself to think about that for the first time in years. He'd denied their existence, cheated them out of their only son. Acknowledging such far-reaching consequences made him feel like a frail ship breaking apart in a storm.

T.S. studied him. He stood so still and quiet. She wished she knew what he was thinking and that she could see his expression in the dark. "You'll probably think I'm crazy when I tell you this, but the week I spent with Moon Man was one of the best times I've ever had."

Logan pulled himself together. "I don't think you're crazy," he forced himself to say over the lump in his throat. Words tumbled desperately without thought from his mouth. "You were a kid. Kids tend to feel deeply. Sometimes they overromanticize situations or endow them with melodrama." Was he speaking about her or himself? "As we get older, we gain more perspective, view things more realistically."

T.S. shook her head. His attitude annoyed her. "Granted, I was young, in love for the first time, and seeing a world I had never seen before. But I don't believe I romanticized or dramatized anything I experienced then. It was real."

Sadness filled her. "As real as the heartbreak of Moon Man betraying me for money," she said, more to herself than him. "I thought he loved me. I guess I was wrong about that."

"What!" Logan almost stopped breathing. The pounding of his heart reached his ears in a deafening roar. An outraged denial screamed through his head. How could she say that? He had loved her, for God's sake!

He stepped closer to her. Saltwater seeped into his shoes, but he was beyond knowing or caring. "What do you mean he betrayed you for money?"

T.S. couldn't stop tears from welling up in her eyes. "One day he took me to the bus station. I thought we were going away together." Her voice caught. "M-my father was waiting for us. He thanked Moon Man for calling him, and he gave him money."

Logan drew her into his embrace, sliding his arms around her waist. "Oh, T.S., I'm sorry," he whispered against her hair.

He ached to tell her how tempted he'd been to take the money, but the look of hurt and disbelief she'd given him had stabbed right into his heart. He'd forgotten how she'd turned away from him and hadn't seen him shove the wadded-up bills back into her father's hand.

A battle raged inside him. Admit the truth or keep silent? He couldn't alter the past. What possible good could it do to tell her the truth now? It wouldn't erase years of hurt, and could only cause them both more grief.

"*I'm* sorry," she murmured, tilting her head back. "I didn't mean to cry all over you. It's just that I've never told anyone about—" She lowered her forehead to his chest. "You must think I'm a complete idiot."

"No, I don't."

"Logan, this morning you said you weren't a kind man. Don't ever try to tell me that again. Because after tonight, I simply wouldn't believe it."

Still torn by the conflicting needs to tell her the truth and to protect the life he'd built, Logan made no reply. He rested his chin on top of her head, simply offering her the comfort of being held, taking consolation himself for the pain of things lost and things impossible.

T.S. leaned into his hard, solid body as if coming home. He squeezed her tight for a moment, then slowly began to massage her back.

Before either of them quite knew what was happening, the comforting turned to desire. T.S. raised her head, and he lowered his mouth to hers. The kiss began so sweetly, but soon changed as their hunger for each other grew. His hands traveled lightly up her back, touching here and there at her spine. She let go of his waist and stretched up on tiptoe to wrap her arms around his neck.

For Logan the kiss was as primeval as the rhythms of the sea. He became oblivious to everything but his burning need for her and the emotional high created by the tiny mewing cries she made.

Goose bumps slithered over T.S.'s skin as their mouths explored each other. She had the sensation that the world had drifted away and all sound had ceased. Heat surged through her as he traced her lower lip with his tongue, teased the sides of her breasts with maddeningly slow caresses.

Logan breathed in her scent and plowed the fingers of one hand into the silky curls lying against her neck. He reached for her hips with his other hand, lifting her up to fit more securely into the cradle of his body. Pressing her tightly to him, he fell to his knees, taking her with him.

He was seconds away from laying her down on the wet sand and loving her until the past was washed clean, when the shock of what he was doing hit him.

"T.S. . . ." His voice came out raspy. He gripped her shoulders and held her at arm's length. Although she didn't move or say a word, he felt her confusion, sensed her questioning gaze upon his face.

As his passion cooled and the primitive beating of his heart slowed, he said, "I'm sorry. I didn't mean for that to happen."

T.S. waited a moment for bittersweet longing to

subside. It didn't. "I'm not sorry. It was wonderful. I've never felt so connected with anyone."

"You were overwrought. Emotionally charged situations tend to distort reality."

"Bull!" she exploded. "I don't need a reality check. I know what I was feeling. I wanted you."

Logan closed his eyes against a tide of renewed desire. He was used to being a cool lover, considerate but in complete command of his passions. T.S. was the only person he'd ever met with the ability to make chaos of his control.

She was so open, so honest. He didn't deserve a woman like her. He had no business wanting her. And he had a life to protect.

Convincing himself that continuing to deceive her was best for both of them, he gently removed his hands from her shoulders and stood up. "Don't make more of it than it is. We're just two strangers who shared a few kisses in the moonlight. It's simply a passing attraction."

She slowly rose to her feet. "Do you really believe that, Logan? Do you?"

He didn't answer. Hurt and disappointment slashed at her soul. She brushed away a tear sneaking down her cheek. He was saying he'd given in to impulse, while it had been the beginning of so much more for her. How ironic, she thought miserably. How very ironic she should always fall for males who didn't seem to want her.

"I wish . . ." he began, and faltered. Wishing was foolish.

"It's all right, Logan." Her voice was a shade too bright. "At least you're honest about your feelings. No harm done." Unless she counted the big crack forming in her heart.

Her words burned through Logan. He felt like a

monster. "I've tried to tell you I'm not a nice man. I'm not someone you want to know."

She knew he'd meant to shock her, and he'd succeeded. Sadly, she realized she'd been right about his wall of fire.

Logan suddenly became aware of the medallion pressing against his skin. The smooth metal had grown heavier and colder. He drew the chain over his head. "I think this necklace belongs to you." He sought her hand in the dark and closed her fingers around the chain.

"You found it!" Her voice was full of relief. "I practically tore the house apart searching for it today. I was going to ask you if I could look for it at your house. You don't know what a relief this is! Thank you."

"It means a lot to you?" he couldn't stop himself from asking.

"More than you'll ever know." T.S. slipped the medallion back into its familiar place and held her hand lovingly over it. She'd missed it. Missed it like an old friend's loving presence.

Logan drew in a ragged breath. He didn't need to question her further to know that a part of her still loved the boy who'd given her the medallion—even though she believed he'd never loved her in return.

"It's getting late," he said. "Let's see if we can get you back into your cottage." He placed his hand on the small of her back to guide her. The courteous gesture felt so intimately possessive, he almost withdrew the touch, but didn't.

As they walked back to the cottages, T.S. didn't know how to break the oppressive silence. Logan was like the Outer Banks—a self-contained, solitary island.

Sighing, she glanced down the strand. A few yards away she saw the wavering beam of a flashlight.

"Look over there," she said, drawing Logan's attention to a child-sized figure scuttling across the strand toward the sand dune. "What do you think he's doing? Chasing ghost crabs?"

"Maybe." Logan was too distracted to speculate on what a child might be doing out alone on the beach so late at night. His mind was busy examining the hollow feeling in his heart.

Jesse Sparrow lay on his stomach in the shadow of the dune. "Close call," he murmured, watching the man and woman disappear from his sight.

He flopped over on his back and cushioned his head with his hands. Eyes too big and too old for his eleven-year-old face stared up at the stars scattered across the sky.

He hadn't worried too much about being seen on this part of the beach, because most of the houses were empty now that school had started. Then, yesterday, that red-haired lady had shown up. She'd moved in across from the deserted cottage where he was holed up in a storage room.

He'd have to be more careful during school hours since there weren't many kids living year-round at this beach. If that lady saw him at the wrong place at the wrong time, she might start wondering what he was doing hanging around.

Jesse was confident he could bluff his way out of any nosy questions the red-haired lady might ask him. Most adults were easy to fool if told a convincing story. Years of practice at explaining away black eyes and broken bones had made him real good at making up stories. But telling lies always made him feel bad.

His stomach rumbled. Jesse wistfully thought of the breakfast hidden among his meager belongings. His mouth watered for the package of peanut-butter crackers he'd stolen from a convenience store while the fat old guy at the cash register was busy talking to a customer. The hamburger, scavenged from a dumpster behind a fast-food place, was less appealing. But hunger made most anything taste good, as long as it didn't smell too vile.

Tomorrow, he'd have to risk another dumpster dive. He had picked up that survival trick from an older kid in Washington, D.C. The stuff grocery stores and restaurants threw away every day amazed him.

He felt a movement near his face and slowly turned his head toward it. A gray-white crab froze inches from his nose. Its little bug eyes stared at him. Then the creature frantically skittered off to bore into the sand.

Jesse wished he were that crab. If anyone tried to hurt him, he could dive into the ground where no one could follow. He wiped the back of his hand on his shirt, then swiped at his eyes, steeling himself against an unfamiliar need to cry.

Cut it out, he told himself. Only babies cried, and he hadn't been a baby for a long time.

He reached for the flashlight and jumped to his feet. Scrambling up the dune, he decided he would head on down to Florida in a day or two. Miami was packed with people. There, Jesse Sparrow would be just another kid in the crowd.

When he reached the top of the dune, he stopped and looked back at the ocean. Yes, sir, that's what he'd do. Truck on down to the land of sunshine, build his sand castles, pretend he lived in them, and never *never* let anyone hurt him again.

The more Jesse thought about that idea, the more he liked it. Florida was a zillion miles away from Maryland and the black-hearted bastard who hated him so much.

Sunday at midmorning, Logan sat on the sunny deck on the upper level of his house. Beside him, the newspaper lay forgotten and a cup of his favorite blend of coffee was untouched. His mind was crowded with thoughts of T.S.

He'd lain awake most of the night, needing her so badly he ached. The intensity of that need terrified him.

Circumstances had made him guarded, and he always kept people at arm's length, never allowing anyone close enough to know the real Logan Hunter. He'd become an expert at holding a tight rein on his emotions. Yet T.S. easily slipped past his guard and pulled emotions out of him by the handful.

Last night, he'd been pitifully inept around her. One minute he'd tried to remain coldly aloof, then the next he'd kissed her like a sex-starved man. He doubted the success of his attempt to warn her away. And in truth, a part of him didn't want her to leave.

He couldn't delude himself into thinking it was only physical desire he felt for T.S. He'd fallen in love with her once. She triggered the same feeling now, but stronger and more difficult to resist.

T.S. Winslow not only threatened the life he'd

built for himself, she was also a serious threat to his emotional equilibrium.

If he wasn't careful, he would want to make a place for her in his life, which was crazy. She was open, honest, warm, and caring. Although she might eventually come to understand why he'd assumed another identity, he doubted someone like T.S. would condone it.

If he was smart, he would forget about potential profit and sell her the damn apartment building.

He turned his gaze to the ocean, and something caught his attention. Squinting against the sun, he got up and looked closer. Brilliant splashes of red, parrot green, topaz yellow, deep turquoise blue, and vivid purple invaded the placid hues of sand, sea, and sky.

It was T.S. moving with languid grace over the beach, an exotic island beauty heading for the water. The breeze teased her hair and molded to her hips the tropical print sarong skirt she wore over a matching swimsuit. Her feet were bare. A canvas bag swung to-and-fro in her hand.

He couldn't take his eyes off the enticing sway of her hips. When she finally stopped at the water's edge, he realized he was holding his breath, and he let it out slowly.

She dropped the bag onto the sand. Raising her arms over her head, she stood on tiptoe, stretching like a sleek, lazy feline in the sunshine. Excitement hummed in Logan's system, vibrating through him like a hard rock beat.

He swallowed painfully. T.S. was a confusing combination of smoldering sensuality and untouchable innocence. She filled his senses, aroused both his passion and protective instincts like no other woman possibly could.

She turned suddenly, as though she felt his gaze upon her. Shading her eyes with one hand, she looked in his direction, then waved at him as if to say, "Come play with me." The floor beneath his feet seemed as unsteady as a ship deck in a storm.

Something inside Logan reached out to her. The feeling grew until he felt like he was drowning in something sweet, intangible, and dangerous. His survival instinct refused to kick in. He had no urge to fight the feeling.

He turned and walked across the deck.

Out on the beach, T.S. watched Logan disappear into his house. He hadn't even returned her wave, she thought with disappointment.

"Well, what did you expect?" she asked herself aloud. The night before the man had as good as said he wasn't interested in her and she should go home.

But she hadn't believed him. The way he'd held her and kissed her told a different story. He wanted her, but he didn't want to want her. T.S. knew if she allowed herself to think about that for long, it would drive her crazy.

Sighing heavily, she fell to her knees and reached for her canvas bag. She spread a towel over the warm sand, then piled on top of it sunscreen, a paperback novel, and a child's plastic pail and shovel.

Determined to forget about the mixed signals Logan Hunter gave off, she set a straw hat on her head and sunglasses on her nose. She was going to enjoy her day at the beach no matter what. Grabbing the pail and shovel, she picked a spot and set about building a sand castle.

Half an hour later, she was absorbed in trying to keep a castle wall from collapsing.

"That's the most haphazard, lopsided thing I've ever seen," Logan said with amusement. "Not even a self-respecting troll would live in it."

Startled, T.S. jerked her head up and at the same time accidentally struck a corner tower with the shovel.

"One tower trashed, three to go," he said, kneeling beside her.

His comment didn't penetrate the sensual fog enveloping her mind. Her gaze drifted over the khaki shirt stretched across his broad shoulders, noting how it hung open to reveal a muscular chest. She followed the fine sprinkling of golden-blond hair covering that chest to where it gradually tapered to a vee and vanished into modest navy swim trunks. The man was simply irresistible, she thought. All tough curves, lean muscles, narrow waist, slim hips, and long, perfectly made legs.

She smiled happily. Happy because he'd come out to be with her. Happily because all of a sudden it was one hell of a beautiful day.

"You just dug another chunk out of the tower," Logan said, closing his hand around hers that held the destructive shovel.

"What?" she whispered, staring into his eyes.

The satiny feel of her skin made him breathless. Instead of removing the plastic tool from her grasp, he found himself lightly tracing the back of her hand with his fingertips.

His gaze settled on her mouth. Intoxicating as strawberries and wine, her lips were only centimeters away. Just a kiss away. Just a . . .

He snatched his hand back. Touching her was

not at all wise. "The tower," he said, picking up the loose thread of conversation. "It's gone."

She lowered her gaze to the castle. "Aw, rats! Double-damn rats. It took me forever to get it up," she said, her voice rising to a disgusted squeak. She sat down hard on the sand and crossly surveyed the damage.

He threw back his head and let out a shout of laughter. It was a rich, full-hearted sound that made T.S. stare at him. He abruptly went silent. A comical expression of surprise formed on his handsome face.

She realized he was as amazed as she over his own merriment. "You look years younger and so carefree when you laugh. I like it. Do it again."

Embarrassed, he shook his head.

"Come on," she coaxed, smiling. "What did I say that was so funny?" Whatever it was, she'd gladly repeat it a million times just to hear him laugh again.

Was he grinning? She took off her sunglasses and peered closely at his mouth. Glory be, he certainly was. And it was a beaut. T.S. felt as if she'd just won the lottery.

Logan fought off a chuckle. Being with her was like setting foot inside a piece of forbidden heaven. "You squeak."

"I beg your pardon?" A puzzled frown arched her brows.

"Sometimes your voice squeaks. Makes you sound like a cartoon mouse." He reached for the pail.

"I do not!" she protested.

"Do too. You just did it again." He examined the figures painted on the plastic bucket. "What are 'Teenage Mutant Ninja Turtles'?"

She laughed. "Pizza-eating crime fighters. Heroes of the under-six set." She settled the sunglasses back on her nose. "Don't you know any children?"

"No. They don't buy real estate," he answered dryly. "Looks like you could use some construction help."

She nodded. "Since you live at the beach, I'll bet you know how to build a great sand castle."

He sprang to his feet, bucket in hand. "Don't bet the farm. You'd lose. I know even less than you do about it. I'll get more water."

"Good idea." She turned to study him as he walked away. It saddened her to think his own laughter surprised him so. What secret sorrows did he keep behind his wall of fire? Before the day was over, she hoped she could make him laugh again.

Logan returned, and they spent an amusing hour working on the castle. At least T.S. was amused and constantly laughing. Logan found the experience exasperating. The wet sand often refused to be molded into the shapes he envisioned. Sometimes she praised his efforts and teased a reluctant smile out of him.

Hunger finally drove them to take a break. Logan ran back to his house for sandwiches and cold drinks.

When the food was gone, T.S. closed her eyes. She stretched out, leaning back on her elbows, enjoying the feel of the wind and mist from the ocean.

Logan's appreciative gaze followed her every move. "Why are you still here?" he asked, looking at the medallion nestled in the valley of her breasts.

"Because I haven't convinced you to sell the

Greensboro property to me." Smiling, she tilted her face up to the sun, and her hat rolled off her head. "And because I like you. Don't ask me why. I'm still working on that."

He took a minute to regain his balance. Her candor was one of the things he liked about her, but he found it emotionally difficult to deal with. "You haven't made a pitch to buy the property today."

"If I did, what would your answer be?" She rolled onto her side and smiled at him.

"I'd say I stand to lose a lot of money if I sold it to you." His dry response made her chuckle.

"That's what I thought you'd say. Relax and enjoy the sun. It's too nice to talk business today."

He scooped up a handful of sand and let it sift through his fingers. "Why is this runaway shelter so important to you that you're willing to finance it yourself? Does it have something to do with your own experience as a runaway?"

"I suppose so, in a way." She sat up and wrapped her arms around her legs. "Runaway children are more of a problem than most people realize. The lucky ones find someone willing to help them. Like I did. Some aren't so fortunate. They live on the street and end up stealing or selling their bodies just to eat. Those are the kids who break my heart. I feel I have a responsibility to them."

She rested her chin on her knees. "There aren't enough shelters for kids who have serious problems with their parents—problems so serious they would rather do anything than go home again. The kind of shelter All Saints wants to create will provide a coordinated program with established community services and with law-enforcement agencies and judicial authorities. The shelter would provide a temporary safe place where kids can receive the assistance they need: a bed, a bath, meals, medical care, counseling. They can seek help without having to worry about being forced to do something they don't want to do. Staff members or volunteers trained in crisis-intervention techniques would be available to them twenty-four hours a day."

"How long can a kid stay?" Logan asked.

"Twenty-four hours to two weeks. I wish we could keep them longer, but that's all the law allows." Her expression became flat, unreadable, as she continued, "The shelter will have a set of rules kids must follow. We are required to notify their families, and we can help arrange counseling through social-service agencies. In a case where child abuse is suspected, the case is handled by protective-service workers. The child is placed in a foster home or in the care of a relative until enough substantiated evidence is gathered to make a final disposition."

"Does it ever get to you?"

"It's been rough at times because we don't have the facilities and trained personnel to deal with these kids." Her eyes clouded for a moment, then she smiled. "But when it does get to me, I just go down to the soup kitchen and spend some time with Mara and the Professor."

"And they are?"

"A bag lady and an often inebriated old man with an unquenchable thirst for poetry." Seeing him shake his head, she laughed. "Mara mothers and bullies me into perking up. Once when I was feeling particularly low, she even let me wear her prized rhinestone tiara. The Professor and I discuss poetry. He favors Tennyson. I'm partial to Shakespeare's sonnets."

Logan's respect for her grew stronger. He realized that when T.S. looked at a person, she saw not the skin, or outer trappings, or what the individual did for a living, but the person inside. That made him wonder what she saw when she looked inside him.

"Our castle needs a name," she said, turning around to admire their handiwork. "I think I'll call it . . . the Kingdom of Vanilla."

He countered her impish grin with a mock scowl. "Is that another wisecrack about my beautiful, professionally decorated home?"

She nodded. He flung a handful of sand at her legs. It was the most spontaneous thing he'd done all day, and she laughed for the joy of it. Watching the harsh line of his mouth soften, she knew there was hope for him after all.

"Would you like to hear a story about the Kingdom of Vanilla?" Not giving him a chance to say no, she plunged in. "Once a upon a time, a prince lived in a castle very much like this one."

"Poor prince," Logan murmured. "He ought to sue the contractors."

She ignored him. "He lived alone in the kingdom he ruled by the sea. The rulers of the surrounding countries constantly bickered with one another. But the prince refused to get involved. Working hard to remain neutral—like Switzerland—the prince banned color from his kingdom, leaving only shades of vanilla and white.

"The prince loved white fish cooked in a white sauce. Every night, the chef prepared the prince's favorite meal, but the prince always went hungry. For it was served to him on a white plate on a white table in a white dining room. You see, the poor prince could never find it in all that whiteness. Hunger made him so grumpy, he never laughed or smiled."

Logan picked up the thread of the story. "Then one evening, the prince answered a knock on the drawbridge door."

"Where was the butler?" she piped up, wondering if she was about to get her comeuppance in his portion of the tale.

"It was his night off. Be quiet and listen."

"Okay, go on."

"A strong wind blew a princess right into his arms. At first, the prince wanted her to go away. You see, he had lived a dull and lonely life for so long, he didn't even know it was dull and lonely. Then the princess began to dazzle him with her brilliant colors, generous spirit, and a smile that must have been a gift from the gods. Her laughter rang through the castle, bringing smiles to solemn faces. Everywhere the princess went, she left splashes of her bright colors. Before the prince realized what was happening, his kingdom was neutral no more."

"Is that the end?" T.S. whispered.

His gaze burned into her. "I . . . don't know."

She leaned toward him. "Maybe it's just the beginning. At least, I'd like to think so."

It was foolish, dangerous even, but Logan silently wished so too. His hand shook as he trailed a finger up her throat, then lifted her chin. Wanting to see her eyes, he removed her sunglasses and tossed them aside.

T.S. put everything she had into the look of longing she gave him. Anticipation hummed through her until it became a song so filled with need that she could no longer wait for him.

She reached for him, digging her nails into his shoulders. "Logan," she sighed, then raised her lips to his.

Without restraint, he kissed her until his senses were so full of her, he could hear only the soft sound of air being taken into her lungs, could feel only the passion ignited by her mouth, could smell only the fragrance of her perfume and the sunscreen on her skin.

The night before, T.S. had thought she was falling for him. Now she knew she had definitely fallen.

A new song sang through her veins. *In love!* Tyler Scott Winslow IV was gloriously, hopelessly, blissfully in *love.*

Overwhelmed by his own emotions, Logan ended the kiss. The intensity of her feelings shone in her eyes and scared the hell out of him. The look was so close to the hero worship she'd once worn for him. It seared him to his soul, and he was reminded of everything that stood between them.

T.S. interpreted the troubled frown furrowing his brows as the forerunner of another apology. Her hands fell away from his shoulders. She stiffened against the bittersweet pain overshadowing her brief moment of happiness.

Lord help him, Logan thought. Why hadn't he locked himself inside his house this morning? Why couldn't he stay away from her?

"T.S.," his voice was a husky rasp. He cleared his throat and started again. "T.S., I'm—"

"Don't say it." She sucked in an angry breath. Her eyes bored into his. "Don't you dare ruin what we just shared by saying you're sorry."

Logan felt like a jerk. He wanted to hold her close, offer tenderness and reassurance, but he was too afraid.

Her anger rapidly cooling, she turned her face toward the sea. She didn't know what to make of him. One minute he was pouring his intensity into kissing her, making her the center of his universe. The next he was shutting her out emotionally, his mouth grim, his eyes hauntingly sad. His unpredictable transitions were as frustrating and baffling as the confusing flashes of *déjà vu* she kept having when she was with him. Never in her life had she felt so off balance.

"I'm not sorry," he said, reclaiming her attention.

With a little sigh she wondered what she was going to do about the mysterious Logan Hunter. She wished she knew what he was truly feeling. Given time and patience, perhaps he would open up to her. But did she have enough of both to reach him?

Suddenly, she needed to get away from him for a few minutes, to be alone to regain her sense of inner balance. "I'm going to look for seashells." She jumped to her feet. "We need them for our castle."

She started to walk away, then stopped to look back at him. Her smile was laced with uncertainty. "You'll wait for me, won't you?"

"I'll wait." He knew he was losing his head. But once again, he didn't care. If she wanted, he'd wait for her forever.

He watched her bend down to pick up a shell. She cupped it in her palm and examined it closely, turning it this way and that with her fingertip.

She walked on. Farther down the strand, she

stopped again. This time, she spoke to a scruffy-looking boy who was diligently working on his own sand castle. Logan saw her kneel down, and he knew she was admiring the child's efforts.

Yes, Logan thought, he would wait for her to come back and show him the treasures she'd found. Wait for T.S.'s enchanting smile and listen to her talk of the small boy she'd just met.

And if he was very lucky, perhaps some of her boundless capacity for the joy of living would renew his jaded soul.

Six

The sand castle drew T.S.'s attention first. It was an intricate work of art, a three-foot magical kingdom with a dragon guarding the entrance.

Then she looked at the boy who had created it. He couldn't have been more than ten, twelve at most. She noticed he was too thin and unkempt. Large brown eyes with thick black lashes were the most arresting feature in his long, hollow-cheeked face.

"Hi," she said.

Head down, a heavy shock of light brown hair falling across one eye, he mumbled something in response.

"My name is T.S. I've never seen such a beautiful sand castle."

The boy's gaze shifted to her face, giving T.S. the impression he might take off like a startled bird should she make any sudden movement.

Her instincts flared to life. She smiled gently. "I'd like to know the name of the artist who created such beauty out of ordinary sand."

An answering smile flickered across his face, as fleeting as a memory. "Jesse."

"I'm glad to meet you, Jesse. I don't know anyone here except my friend, Logan. He lives here. I'm just visiting for a while. I'm staying in that little cottage up there." She pointed it out to him. "I wouldn't mind having another friend to talk to sometimes, so feel free to stop by whenever you want. If you get too hot or hungry out here and home is too far away, I won't mind if you knock on my door. I don't lock the cottage during the day. Grab a drink or something to eat. I won't mind." She had been keeping the door locked during the day, but now she wouldn't. Just in case her instincts were right.

He scanned her face, searching for truth. T.S. looked directly into his eyes, hoping he would find it there.

The next two days dragged by for T.S. Nothing seemed to be going right. The crew at All Saints was pleading for her to come back. Her father had phoned twice, demanding she return home by the coming weekend to attend a business dinner with him. She was no closer to convincing Logan to sell the Greensboro property than she was to finding out how he truly felt about her.

Her progress with Jesse was slow, too, and sometimes agonizing. It was like trying to tame a frightened wild creature that had no reason to trust a human being. But she thought she was beginning to build a foundation of trust between herself and the child.

The boy hadn't been brave enough to knock on her door yet. Nothing, no food or money, had been missing from the cottage, so she knew he hadn't been there in her absence.

Twice, she had talked to him on the beach in the afternoon while he sculpted his sand castles. She had done most of the talking, mostly about safe or inconsequential things. She told him about spending every summer with her mother at the beach, and how her father had sold the beach house when her mother had died. In response, the boy had spoken of his own mother, who had died when he was four. She hadn't pressed him for details, and he hadn't offered any.

Both times, she had pretended she was hungry and had insisted on running back to her cottage for cold drinks and sandwiches. She'd also pretended not to notice the way he tried to eat slowly and savor every bite.

The unresolved problems hanging over her head with both Jesse and Logan made T.S. more conscious of the clock ticking away than she'd ever been in her life.

By Wednesday morning, she was feeling restless and reckless. She was tired of seeing Logan only for a few hours at the end of his long workdays. Their couple of dinners out and the midnight walks on the strand were all very nice. But she wanted more than friendly conversations and kisses that practically set her hair on fire.

Time was running out, and she knew she wasn't staying in Nags Head in hopes of buying the apartment building. If necessary, she could find another place for the runaway shelter. It might not be as perfectly located as the one she wanted, but it could be done.

She was staying because of Logan. What she couldn't find was another man like him. Until she had met him, she hadn't even known she'd been looking for him. T.S. was certain her strong feelings of familiarity with him was a sign that he was the man for her. Logan made her feel the same kind of emotional connection and intensity she had experienced with her first love. She simply had to know if there was any chance of a permanent relationship between them.

Planning to take the owner of Hunter Properties by surprise and shake him up a lot, she got dressed and left the cottage.

Logan was in his office, heavily involved in putting together next year's rental brochure. Hearing his door suddenly burst open, he glanced up with a frown. His secretary blocked the threshold with her six-foot, solidly built body.

"Young lady, you just hold it right there!" Mrs. Midgett's stern voice could have scared a drill sergeant out of his combat boots. "I told you, Mr. Hunter is a very busy man. He cannot be disturbed, and that's that. If you want to talk to another agent, fine. Go park the seat of your pants on a chair, and I'll see who's available."

Logan swallowed a groan, wishing public relations were as high on Mrs. Midgett's priority list as protecting his privacy. "Is there a problem, Mrs. Midgett?"

"Hi, Logan," T.S. called out cheerfully, snaking her hand past his robust secretary to wave at him. "Mamie and I are just having a slight disagreement."

His mouth dropped open, and he quickly closed it.

Mamie? He doubted even Mr. Midgett had permission to use his wife's first name.

"It's all right, Mrs. Midgett," he said. "Ms. Winslow is a . . ." He hesitated in confusion. T.S. was the woman he loved, but he'd rather go naked in public than admit that aloud. "A friend." Yes, that would do nicely, he thought, nodding to himself.

Turning sideways, Mamie Midgett folded her arms over her ample bosom and stared at the phenomenal event taking place before her very eyes. The cute little thing she'd had so much fun arguing with for the past ten minutes danced right up to Logan Hunter, kissed him on the mouth, then plopped her fanny down on his desk. Mamie had been with the boss since the first day he'd opened Hunter Properties, and she'd never thought she'd live to see any female make him look so flustered and goofy-eyed.

Mamie pursed her lips to keep from grinning. She silently blessed the persistent Ms. Winslow for coming along to save her boss from making a big mistake with that twitter-patted Melissa. In her opinion Logan Hunter needed someone sweet and vivacious like this little redhead, not a woman with a mercenary heart and press-on nails.

As soon as the door softly closed behind his secretary, Logan scooted his chair back. He smiled at T.S. She smiled back at him bright as the morning sun, eyes shining like blue gemstones. Looking at her, he was suddenly aware that the deep loneliness he sometimes felt was banished whenever he was with her.

"Hi," she said softly.

"Hi, yourself." He eyed her shiny red, white, and blue American-flag T-shirt and red shorts. "Twenty years ago, that shirt could have gotten you a close acquaintance with a jail cell."

She laughed, crossing one white tennis shoe and red sock–shod foot over the other. "Times have changed. I'm showing patriotic support for my country."

Logan's mind turned back to the time his father had been arrested for wearing a flag sewn on the back of his jeans. "Wipe that grin off yer face, boy. Don't cha know it's un-American to sit on the flag of these here U-nited States?" the deputy sheriff from the small mountain town nearest the commune had said as he slapped a pair of handcuffs on Sean Chase's wrists.

And maybe he was changing as well, Logan realized with a jolt of amazement. Thinking about that incident now amused rather than embarrassed him.

"So, this is where you do your real estate thing," she said, glancing curiously around his office.

Logan tried to see it through her eyes. The stark black, white, and gold furnishings he'd always considered simplistically elegant now seemed austere. No pictures on his desk. No plants. Not even so much as a paper clip out of place. She was the only splash of color and distraction in the room.

He switched his gaze to the smooth, tanned length of her legs. "Not that I'm not glad to see you, but what are you doing here?"

"I've come to take you away from all this. I'm kidnapping you." She gave him one of the dazzling smiles he was rapidly coming to crave.

A smile flirted with his mouth too. "And just how are you planning to do that, Ms. Winslow?"

Without breaking eye contact, T.S. slowly inched off the black marble–topped desk. She bent down to drape her arms around his shoulders. "I'm going to tell you I missed you today," she whispered, sliding her hands up to caress the back of his neck.

A shiver of anticipation ran through him. "Is that all?"

"Then I'm going to tell you I want you. Don't you think we've waited long enough?"

He sat very still, mesmerized by the sound of her voice and the sight of her tongue wetting her lips. His palms grew moist as he tightly gripped the chair arms. "And if that doesn't work?"

"I'm going to kiss you like this." She began a slow, deliberate seduction, kissing the tip of his chin, then working her way up to his eyes. Finally, she sought out his mouth and parted his lips with her tongue. A lazy exploratory kiss swiftly changed, bursting into hungry desire.

Pure pleasure exploded inside Logan's head. He released his white-knuckled grip on the arms of his chair and reached for her, pulling her down onto his lap. His hand skimmed over her taut stomach to the swell of her hips, then traveled down to explore her satiny thigh.

Heat worked its way up T.S.'s torso with his touch. The sweet magic of his hand on her breast produced a soft moan. Primitive passion overtook what she'd begun as an effort to tease him away from his work.

How right she had been. Logan Hunter was a man surrounded by a wall of fire, and yet as comfortably familiar to her as her own image. She wouldn't mind burning with him forever.

She lifted her head and exhaled an unsteady breath. "How do you do it?" she asked with a trace of awe.

"Do what?" he answered, brushing his thumb over her aroused nipple.

"Make me feel like I've always loved you."

His hand fell away from her breast. Her candid

confession ripped at Logan's heart, revealing a dark secret he had never acknowledged before. It was an appalling belief that he didn't deserve to be loved, therefore rendering him incapable of truly loving anyone in return.

T.S. saw a stricken expression in the depths of his hard blue eyes, and her spirits sank. He might want her, but he didn't want her love. She slowly released her hold on him, letting her hands drift down to lie pressed together in her lap.

"Obviously, you didn't want to know I love you." She lowered her head. God, she was only making things worse! "It's okay, you don't have to love me back. I mean, I wish you could. But if you don't, you don't. I can accept that. I'm not good at hiding my feelings. Never have been. Never will be. My father says I'm too emotional. He thinks it's a character defect. Maybe he's right. I'm babbling. I'm so embarrassed."

Logan put his hand under her chin and raised her face to meet his gaze. "I realize I didn't react as you may have hoped. Please understand, I do care about you. It's just that I'm not as comfortable with emotions as you are. I've never had much faith in them, I guess."

The tenderness in his voice, the look in his eyes, warmed T.S. and gave her hope. He *did* care. Maybe he just needed someone to teach him how to love the way he needed someone to teach him how to laugh.

He dragged his thumb across her lower lip. "And I think your father is wrong. I don't believe there's a single defect in your character. You're the best person I've ever known. Without demanding anything in return, you give affection from a great wellspring of generosity. Like a gift from the sea, it's simply there, offered freely."

She placed the palm of one hand on his cheek. "That's the most wonderful thing anyone has ever said to me. Thank you. I feel much better now. In fact, I almost feel better than the time Mara let me wear her tiara."

"Ah, yes, Mara-the-bag-lady. Genuine rhinestone tiaras aren't easy to top, I suppose?"

She traced the conservative pattern of his tie as she pretended to consider the matter. "Well, I don't know. The tiara was very sparkly. I like sparkly things."

"I'll keep that in mind. What do I have to do to compete with something sparkly?"

Mischief danced in her eyes. "Abandon your stuffy office for a whole day of fun adventures with me."

"I couldn't do that. Mrs. Midgett would be too shocked," he said, although he knew he would end up doing anything T.S. wanted him to do.

"Give her the rest of the day off." She loosened his tie. "It will do her good. Why do you call her Mrs. Midgett?"

"Because she told me to. I asked her what I should call her the day I hired her. She fixed her steely eyes on me and said, 'Mrs. Midgett, of course.' She terrifies me, and she knows it."

The thought of Logan Hunter being terrified of anyone made her laugh so hard, she almost fell off his lap.

Two hours later, suit jacket stripped off and shirtsleeves rolled up, Logan stood at the summit of Jockey's Ridge. For the first time since he'd left his office with T.S., he wished he were back there.

Lunch had been fun. Browsing through shops with her had sort of been fun too—even though he hated shopping. He'd been secretly pleased when she bought him a mood ring, but had flatly refused a T-shirt imprinted with the words CAPTAIN CONDOM SAYS, 'WRAP THAT RASCAL.'

But this, Logan thought, looking straight down into the marshy waters of Roanoke Sound, this was not fun.

He checked his mood ring and saw it was gray-black—an indication of unhappiness or stark terror. No doubt he was crazy as well. What color would it turn when he lay broken and bleeding at the bottom of this vast sand hill?

Trying to remember everything the instructor had said about thermals and ridge-lift air currents, he glanced over at a radiant-faced T.S. A harness was being attached to her waist. She looked as if she were wearing a giant colorful kite. And in a moment *he* would be strapped to one of those contraptions.

He felt a little sick to his stomach, thinking about jumping off the top of the hill with nothing but air and a fixed-wing glider between him and instant death. He put on his crash helmet. At least his brains wouldn't get splattered all the way to Kitty Hawk.

The instructor came over to strap him into his glider. The young man cast a dubious look at him and said, "You'll be okay if you don't panic. Just relax, remember your instructions, and have fun."

"This is going to be great!" T.S. was so thrilled, she practically squeaked. Her eyes shone like a child's on Christmas morning. She blew Logan a kiss and started her run down into the wind.

He wished he could share her excitement. It was difficult to work up much enthusiasm, though, when he was certain he was literally about to bite the dust along with his favorite suit pants.

"I am one with the glider," he murmured, pumping his feet into the sand, starting his own downhill run.

"I am one with air." The wind lifted a little of the kite's burden from his back.

"I am one big idiot!" he yelled as he was suddenly jerked off his feet. Eyes clenched shut, he hovered motionless over the slope for a heart-pounding, helpless instant.

Then the glorious miracle of flight kicked in. Logan opened his eyes. *He was flying!* Like the Wright brothers. Like a bird. Soaring noiselessly, weightlessly, he was no longer an earthbound man. He knew just how the Greek mathematician Archimedes had felt twenty-two centuries ago when he jumped out of his bath and rushed down the street crying, "Eureka!"

Quickly, Logan settled into the quiet command of piloting the glider, delicately adjusting to nature's currents. His view was taken up by a sky that deepened in blue and thinned out to white as it stretched toward the horizon. He'd once read that wide-open spaces were associated with freedom and adventure, and he suddenly understood why it was so.

Shifting his weight to the right dipped the right wing, and he turned in that direction, searching the sky for T.S.

He dragged air into his lungs when he saw her. She was a vision of brilliantly colored wings flashing in the sunlight. Fascinated, he watched her ascend, descend, and circle with the ease of a graceful butterfly.

Never, he thought, had her inner harmony seemed so apparent. She was totally at peace with herself. He both envied and loved her for that, because the darker side of life never seemed to overshadow the delight she found in simply being alive.

It was then that he made his decision. He would tell her the truth and give her the Greensboro property she wanted. She might hate him for his deception, but it was a risk he would have to take. It was the right thing to do—an atonement for the past grief he had inflicted upon her and for that which was to come.

But he wouldn't tell her just yet. He was selfish enough to want another day of her loving him.

All too soon it was time to land. He came in low into the wind and pushed the control bar out. The glider stalled.

Logan dropped to his feet, becoming earthbound once more.

"What color is your mood ring, Logan?" T.S. asked, still feeling high from the exhilaration of hang gliding.

"Happy."

Laughing, she stood on tiptoe to press a quick, hard kiss on his mouth. Then she danced away, heading for the ice-cream parlor across the street from Jockey's Ridge.

"What's next on your fun agenda?" he called, following at a more sedate pace. "Shark wrestling?"

She smiled at him over her shoulder. "We're going to celebrate."

"If we can do it sitting down, I'm game."

She stopped and turned around. Waiting for him to catch up with her, she studied him. His suit jacket was hooked on one finger and slung over his shoulder. That morning, he'd gone off to work dressed conservatively for success. Now he looked windblown, rumpled, and absolutely divine.

"Feet hurt?" she asked sympathetically as he reached her.

He nodded, sending a shock of hair falling into his eyes. Reaching up, he impatiently flipped it away from his forehead.

The back of T.S.'s neck prickled. In a flash she was sixteen again, standing with Moon Man on the sidewalk of an unfamiliar city in the unforgiving heat of summer. His long golden hair flowed around his shoulders and fell down into his eyes.

Feeling unsettled, she gazed up at Logan. Had he actually used the same gesture, the same flick of the wrist and fingers, to toss his hair out of his eyes? Was her imagination simply playing tricks on her? Was she subconsciously trying to make him fit her fantasy of a lost love?

These strange episodes of familiarity had to stop, she told herself firmly. Okay, so he reminded her in some ways of Moon Man. But Logan was Logan. Uniquely himself.

She realized he was speaking to her. Shrugging off her quirky thoughts, she smiled. "I'm sorry. What did you say?"

"These shoes were not meant for climbing sand hills or chasing after wild redheaded women," he repeated. "What are we going to celebrate with?"

"Frozen yogurt."

One corner of his mouth lifted into a slight smile. "Double dutch chocolate?"

"Of course. My treat." She took his arm, and they leisurely strolled toward the shopping complex.

Logan was easily persuaded to wait on a bench outside the ice-cream shop while T.S. went inside. After checking out all the various flavors and toppings just for fun, she ordered two cups of low-fat chocolate yogurt.

She was on her way out of the shop when she glanced through the window. "Jesse," she murmured in surprise.

The boy stood in front of Logan. A mechanical smile in place, Jesse's mouth worked rapidly. T.S. was disturbed by his appearance, which was even more unkempt than the day she'd met him on the beach. Tiredness was etched into his face like a permanent condition. He was holding his hand out, palm up in supplication.

With a sense of foreboding she stepped closer to the window. She watched Logan pick up his suit jacket, paw through an inner pocket, and come out with his business card and a twenty-dollar bill. The boy eagerly accepted both, stuffing them into his shirt as if afraid Logan might suddenly change his mind.

Heart in her throat, T.S. knew her suspicions about Jesse had just been confirmed. He was on his own. It was possible he had been abandoned, but her instincts told her he was a runaway.

Just then, the boy looked up and met her gaze through the glass. T.S. saw the spare widening of his eyes, the intake of his breath, the startled ightening of his shoulders, the brief flash of shame coloring his pasty cheeks.

Every impulse of humanity called for her to rush out to him, but she knew he would only take off like a frightened bird. Common sense called for her to practice restraint. She smiled at him, pouring into that smile every ounce of compassion and understanding she possessed.

Jesse turned and fled.

She swallowed her disappointment, telling herself he knew where to find her. When he was ready, he would come to her.

It had happened before with runaways she had encountered on the streets. She'd lost track of the number who had come looking for her both at home and at the All Saints office.

T.S. didn't know what she said or did that inspired trust in such kids. Maybe it was their own sixth sense that told them she was someone who genuinely cared about their welfare. Maybe she unconsciously gave off signals that invited their confidence. Whatever it was, she hoped it didn't fail her now.

Leaving the shop, she went out and sat down on the bench beside Logan.

"Thank you." He accepted the treat she handed him and dug into it as if he hadn't eaten in a week.

"I noticed you were talking to a boy a few minutes ago. What was that all about?" She took a bite of frozen yogurt, though she'd lost her appetite for it.

"Nothing really," he said, shrugging. "The kid was panhandling."

Curious to see if he would admit it, she asked, "Did you give him money?"

He met her gaze. "Of course not," he said, then serenely spooned more yogurt into his mouth, like a man without so much as a smudge to mar his conscience. "Kids have no business begging on the streets. If they want money, let 'em work for it." He wagged his white plastic spoon at her. "We can't all be bleeding-heart do-gooders like you, Ms. Winslow."

"Oh, pardon me, Mr. Scrooge, I forgot you're supposed to be mean and hard." A secret smile warmed her from the inside out. Obviously, he was a man who preferred to conduct his benevolences with discretion and without sentiment.

"Do try to keep that in mind." His voice was as light and teasing as hers had been.

What a wonderful, intriguingly contradictory man she'd chosen to fall in love with, T.S. thought. His life was his work. Yet he'd easily allowed her to convince him to play hooky. His home was decorated in a neutral, emotionless style, and in that environment he listened to music from a colorful era highly charged with emotion. He professed to be hard and uncaring, but he treated her with kindness and tenderness. And he'd given Jesse a twenty-dollar bill.

She stole a peek at Logan. He might not know it, but his heart was as deep and wide as the Atlantic Ocean. How could she not love a man like him? The smile that had been warming her on the inside finally reached her lips and turned into a delighted grin.

Eyes stinging with humiliation, Jesse weaved through the crowd of people strolling from store to store. He felt as if everyone were looking at him. Looking and knowing. Knowing he was a beggar, a liar, a thief. A boy so bad his own father didn't want him around anymore.

He left the shopping complex behind, running toward the sea. On he ran, lungs fighting for breath, legs weak, stomach churning.

Finally, he reached the sand dune overlooking the strand. There he collapsed, head down for a moment. Then he sat with his knees drawn up to his chin, hands gripping his legs for something to hold on to.

Why? Why did T.S. have to see him begging? Shame crawled up his spine.

She always spoke to him so nicely. Something in him desperately wanted to trust the kindness he saw in her pretty blue eyes, but he had learned a long time ago not to trust anyone.

Jesse shuddered and drew in a ragged breath. She said he was a sand artist. She gave him food. In his imagination she lived in his castles too.

Would she hate him now?

He stayed on the dune, feeling *very* small and *very* alone, watching the gulls dip, wheel, and dive in the air.

After reluctantly parting with T.S. at the door of her cottage at four-thirty, Logan went home to shower and change. In an hour he was to meet her for an early dinner and a game of miniature golf.

Out of habit he walked into the kitchen to check his answering machine. Frowning, he tossed his jacket on the breakfast bar and gazed indecisively at the red message light. The calls he usually received were business-related. His fingers hovered over the Rewind and Play buttons.

Did he really want to know what he'd missed today while he was playing hooky from work with T.S.? Knowing would only make him feel guilty and negligent.

"To hell with it," he murmured, turning his back on the ominous red light. For the first time in he didn't know how long, he was too full of good feelings to allow guilt to intrude. Why ruin it? If there was a price to pay for it, he'd deal with it later.

He took a moment to root through his music collection. The Doors. Janis Joplin. Crosby, Stills, Nash, & Young. None of them suited his mood. He grinned as he glanced down at the cheap oval ring on his finger. It was still the blue-green of happiness.

Continuing his search, he chose a CD with a selection of Bob Seger songs recorded in concert. He turned the stereo system on, then cranked up the music to an earsplitting volume parents were always warning their kids about—though his parents never had. "Night Moves" practically vibrated off the walls.

Logan headed for the bathroom, listening to Seger's smoky voice sing about hot summer nights and teenagers practicing night moves in a '60 Chevy. That was something else he'd missed out on as a young teenager. Since he lived in a commune with more than a dozen uninhibited adults, sex had never been much of a mystery to him. And even though a few girls he'd known at school would have been willing, he'd been too embarrassed to invite them to crawl in back of a VW van painted like a hippie's bad trip. What he'd wanted then was the kind of life he'd only seen in *Leave It to Beaver* reruns.

With the echoes of missed opportunities and hot summer nights ringing in his head, he stripped off his clothes and stepped into the shower. One long, steamy night in Richmond, Virginia, was particularly on his mind. He remembered lying awake on the sofa in Jack's tiny apartment, watching T.S. sleep in the single bed across the room. *Night moves.* Watching and wanting . . .

When he came out again, Seger had launched into a song about loneliness and love.

Was T.S. as lonely as he was? Selecting a shirt that was almost as deep a blue as her eyes, he slipped it on and tucked it into charcoal-gray pants. Would they have tonight? The one he'd wanted sixteen years ago, the one he wanted even more now?

If she could forgive and accept him as he was, was it possible they could have tomorrow?

Dressed in a peach silk bustier and matching panties, T.S. eyed her depressingly meager choices hanging in the closet. The sea-green suit she'd worn to Logan's office the day she arrived was wrinkled beyond redemption and inappropriate anyway. The only other possibility was her all-purpose, short, black jersey sheath.

Sighing, she removed the garment from the hanger and put it on, then slipped her feet into the basic black flats she'd packed to go with the dress. Turning to the dresser, she chose a pair of dangling silver teardrop earrings to wear with her crescent-moon and stars medallion.

Stepping back, she critically examined herself

in the mirror. It wasn't exactly the look she wanted, but it would have to do. At least her underwear would make Logan's temperature rise. The grin on her face vanished. If they got that far, she thought, turning to leave the room. Given his frustrating on-again-off-again behavior, she couldn't take anything for granted.

In the kitchen she poured a glass of iced tea and drank it while absently staring out the window over the sink. As she waited for Logan to arrive, she felt as if she'd been waiting for someone all her life. Not just for any someone, but for him. Unfortunately, she wasn't so sure *he* had been waiting for her.

Love wasn't what she had expected to find when she came to Nags Head. She hadn't been looking for it, but she accepted it the way she accepted the fact that she had red hair and blue eyes.

She didn't know what love meant to Logan. More than likely, it was just another emotion he didn't trust. To her it meant an intensely physical, emotional, and spiritual union of two different and separate people who contributed to each other, allowing the space and freedom for growth, not only as a unit but as individuals as well.

Apprehension coursed through her. Did she want too much? Was she being overly optimistic in believing she could break through Logan's wall of fire?

Her confidence took a dive. Maybe she did have a fatal character flaw, one that drew her to men incapable of returning her love.

Setting the glass on the counter, she started to turn away when a movement caught her eye. She leaned closer to the window and saw a figure bent low, running swiftly along the gravel and shell-strewn road. Before she could do more than register that it was Jesse, he had disappeared into the storage room in the carport beneath the cottage directly across from hers.

Seven

She was much too quiet, Logan thought. She'd hardly spoken a word on the way to the restaurant. Now she was too preoccupied to give much attention to the view of the sunset over Roanoke Sound, or the artifacts and memorabilia from the S.S. *United States* that the Windmill Point restaurant was famous for. She'd barely touched her dinner. T.S. simply wasn't acting like herself.

And she'd shed her bright colors. That bothered him almost as much as her somber mood and her polite responses to his conversational attempts. Where were her vibrant colors? Where was her startling candor that kept him confused, off balance, and fascinated?

Wishing he could see into her mind, Logan studied the perfect shape of her head, bent thoughtfully downward. She seemed so far away, so inaccessible to him, and he didn't like it.

Intent on getting to the bottom of her perplexing mood, he reached out and laid his hand possessively over hers. "You're very quiet tonight."

"Am I?" She switched her gaze to him. Her blue eyes, ivory skin, and auburn hair were made all the more striking by the long sleeved, form-fitting black dress she wore.

It was a great dress, he thought, but it was black. His gaze traveled from the silver earrings dangling from her shell-like ears to the ivory column of her throat, then lingered a moment on the gentle swell of her breasts, and the medallion nestled in the valley between them.

"Is something wrong, T.S.?" he asked, watching her face carefully.

She smiled, but it was a distracted smile. "Nothing really. I was just lost in thought." *Thinking about their relationship, thinking about Jesse.*

"About what?"

T.S. regarded him pensively, debating whether to tell him about Jesse or not. It was one thing for her to know the whereabouts of a runaway child and not report it to the police. She knew the risks involved in harboring a runaway minor, and she accepted those risks. It was another thing to know Jesse had broken into the storage room of a cottage owned or in the care of Hunter Properties.

How would Logan react to the situation? Would he insist on contacting the police? She couldn't blame him if he did. Yet as much as she tried not to place unfair expectations on other people, she knew she would be very disappointed if he did want to call the police.

T.S. hated moral dilemmas. "The cottage directly in back of mine," she said hesitantly. "It's one of your rentals, isn't it?"

"Yes. It's also for sale. Are you interested?"

"Spoken like a true salesman." She laughed and was glad to see him smile in response. Smiles seemed to be coming more easily to him these last few days. Unfortunately, she had a feeling she was about to wipe that wonderful smile right off his face.

"Logan, I believe the little boy I was talking to Saturday on the beach—" She broke off and swallowed hard. Telling someone something he wasn't going to like was the pits. Even worse, there was no way to ease him into the situation. She sighed and began again. "You met him earlier today, after we went hang gliding. He was the kid who asked you for money. His name is Jesse. He's a runaway, and he's living in the storage room in the house I asked you about."

Flat silence stretched between them. T.S. anxiously studied his face, trying to gauge his reaction. He was as unreadable as a book with the pages glued together.

Logan sat back. "I see."

She stared at him. "That's it? That's all you're going to say?"

"How long have you known about this?" He could see she was surprised that he didn't seem upset about it. It occurred to him that she had been reluctant to tell him because she didn't quite trust him to want to help the child. That hurt, but he knew he had set himself up for it.

"I've suspected he was on his own for several days now," she said in answer to his question. "But I didn't know where he was holed up until just before you picked me up for dinner. I was standing by the window in the kitchen, and I saw him go into the storage room."

"You know he can't stay there, don't you?"

"I know," she said, feeling sick at heart. "I don't blame you for wanting to call the police."

Logan's brows rose a fraction. "I didn't say anything about calling the police."

She could have kissed him. "I love you, Mr. Scrooge. You did give Jesse money. I saw you."

He shrugged. "So, I'm a sucker for hungry kids." He remembered all too well what it was like. "I take it you have some sort of plan in mind?"

"I've talked to him several times, and I think he's beginning to trust me. I'm waiting for him to ask for help. When he does, I'll give it to him."

"What if he doesn't ask?"

"He will."

Logan shook his head. "T.S., as much as I hate to say it again, I cannot allow that boy to stay where he is indefinitely."

"Just give him a couple more days, please?" She reached across the table and grasped his hand.

"Two days." He turned her hand palm up and ran his finger along her lifeline. "If he doesn't come to you by then, either you go get him or I will."

A brilliant smile lit up her face, but quickly faded as she realized Logan now shared the risks. "Harboring a runaway is against the law, punishable by two years in jail and/or a fine. I don't know if our knowing about Jesse and not reporting it immediately is the same thing as harboring, but it very well could be. I don't want to cause trouble for you."

Logan was touched by her genuine concern for him. It almost canceled out the hurt he felt at her lack of trust. The irony of the situation wasn't lost on him either. The princess didn't mind taking the consequences of her own little civil disobedience, but she was worried about getting him—a man she considered a law-abiding straight arrow—

involved in something that could be construed as illegal.

"I understand," he said, wondering why he wasn't laughing or crying over the absurdity. "I can take the heat. Was that all that was on your mind?"

"No," she admitted. "I was also thinking about you and me."

"Which subject do you want to tackle first?" He laced his fingers with hers. "Personally, I prefer to talk about you."

T.S. managed a shaky smile. "I've noticed that." He was so adamant about slamming the door closed on anything to do with his past or emotional issues. But she needed more than he'd been willing to give her so far. She needed to know if the possibility of commitment between them was out of the question.

"I don't mind telling you anything you want to know," she said, and squeezed his hand. "I love you, and I want to know more about you. Regardless of what you might think, I won't be shocked or upset by whatever lies behind the wall you surround yourself with. You can't imagine some of the things people have told me about themselves." Her voice was so soft, it seemed to drift across his skin like a night breeze. "I'm asking you to trust me. Help me, Logan, help me get over the wall."

Anger prickled up his spine. She just kept picking away at his veneer, forcing him to face his past and reexamine his life. Even though his childhood memories didn't seem as painful as they once had, he couldn't tell her what she wanted to know without also telling her the truth about his identity.

"My past isn't important." He hated himself for saying that, but he wasn't ready to reveal his secrets. Not here. Not now. He also knew he'd hate himself even more if he complicated matters further by reciting more of his fabricated background.

"If it troubles you so much that it's hard for you to talk about it, then it *is* important," she gently persisted. "Start with something easy. Tell me what you were like as a child."

Something easy? He withdrew his hand from hers as alternating heat and cold raced through him. "I was breast-fed on ideals I couldn't share, given space and freedom when I wanted structure and discipline." His voice dropped and his muscles tightened.

From his expression, T.S. knew he was no longer looking at her but inside himself. She didn't realize she was holding her breath until he spoke again.

"I hated school but liked learning. I did extra-credit projects and made the best grades. Because I was different, smaller, and not allowed to play sports, I didn't fit in with the other kids. Teachers gave me hell for anything that went wrong, and for fights I didn't start but refused to walk away from. In short, I was loner." The warning gleam in his eyes made it clear he was finished and the subject was now closed.

The picture he painted of a lonely, confused childhood touched her heart. "You wanted a different life than the one you had," she said softly. "I can understand that because so did I. Perhaps we have more in common than we know."

"What kind of kid were you?"

"Always wanting to please. I did everything I was told to do because I was afraid that if I didn't, my father wouldn't approve of me. In short," she said, repeating his own words with a quick grin, "I was obedient."

"A trait you unfortunately outgrew." His mournful tone made her laugh. "Are you still trying to earn your father's approval?" he asked curiously, never having had to deal with his parents as an adult.

She shook her head. "No. When I was growing up, the lines between love and approval were blurred. My father doesn't know how to show love, but he knows how to show approval and disappointment. It took me a long time to learn to live with the fact that I will always have his love but never his approval."

Logan cast his mind back sixteen years. When they'd walked into that bus station, Tyler Winslow had impressed him as a coldly rigid man, and for an instant he had worried he'd done the wrong thing in contacting him. Then the man had looked at T.S. with the eyes of a worried father, and Logan had known it would be all right to give her back into his care.

"Would you mind if we skipped miniature golf?" she asked.

"What would you like to do instead?" he asked, signaling to the waitress.

She grinned. "Go home with you. We can look at the stars from your deck and talk a little. When we're tired of that, you can take my hand, lead me into the house, and kiss me like you mean it."

As he took in the significance of her words, Logan's heart began to thump erratically. He cleared his throat, pretending not to be affected. "Sounds good to me."

He paid the bill, and they left the restaurant.

During the short drive back to his house, he grew increasingly agitated. Desire ran hot and heavy through his veins, and his thoughts ran in a vicious cycle. Making love with T.S. without telling her who he was wouldn't be right. But if he told her, he didn't believe she would still want him. Once he made love with T.S., he wouldn't want to let her go. When he told her who he was, she wouldn't want to stay.

Logan Hunter knew he was in one hell of a mess.

T.S. had the notion Logan would take a nosedive over the handrail if she goosed him. He was acting jumpier than a cat contemplating a close encounter with a litter box filled with hot coals.

Love, desire, and—heaven help her—amusement grew tight inside her chest as she followed Logan up the two flights of steps to the second level of his house. No, please, no, she told herself. Don't laugh at him. It would wound his pride too much if he knew she was amusingly aware of his unusual display of nervous tension.

By the time they reached the deck, T.S. had subdued the threat of laughter. When he turned and met her gaze, she let him see the love and desire she felt.

Neither of them moved for a moment. They stood looking at each other in the dying sunlight. Only the sound of the tide's encroaching waves and the cry of gulls overhead broke the silence between them.

"Well, here we are," he finally murmured.

"Yes, here we are."

He glanced up at the haze of purple in the sky. "Too early for stars."

"You're right," she said, lessening the distance

between. Deep in her soul she knew they were meant to be together. "Not a star in sight. What shall we do?"

A smile curved her mouth. Looking at him now with his vulnerability exposed, she wondered how she could ever have considered his face too harsh and unyielding. His attack of nerves was as endearing as his intensity was exciting.

She stood so near. Logan could breathe in the fragrance clinging to her skin, and see the soft appeal in her exquisite eyes. Dusk seemed to whisper through her hair, and he wanted to capture the feel of its coppery sheen with his fingers.

"So here we are," she said again. Her voice was low and smoky, and he heard it through a misty veil of longing. "Kiss me, Logan. Kiss me like you mean it."

"Yes." It was all he could manage to say, because his gaze had narrowed until only the delicate contours and velvet softness of her face filled his vision and his mind.

He raised one hand and touched her cheek, and she saw his eyes take on a languid expression. His fingertips caressed her face, altering pressure, seeking sensitive nerve points. Heat surged beneath her skin, and she had to steady herself against the tremors invading her body.

Everything she wanted was there in his eyes, and beat within her heart. Framing his face between her palms, she brought his mouth down to hers. She felt the quickening of his breath just before their lips met in a poignant kiss. His mouth opened, letting her seek the intimacy she wanted so badly.

Her fingers slid upward and wove through his hair, feeling its silky thickness as she repeatedly sifted it through her spread fingers. Loving him with deep certainty, she pressed closer, silently offering herself into his keeping.

With his lips drinking in her adoration, he began a sensual worship with his hands, traveling with light friction over her jersey dress. Hot runners of pleasure weakened her knees, and she had to hold on to his shoulders to keep from sinking bonelessly down to his feet.

She whispered his name, and it sounded like a prayer. Her lips sought his square jaw and the sensitive skin beneath it.

Love and desire too long denied rioted in Logan's body. Mind free-floating with every fervent sensation, he tried to communicate with his hands the aching tenderness he felt for her. Gathering her into his embrace, he lifted and fitted her against him. Palm flat, fingers spread, he skimmed his hand down her back to curve around her bottom.

He kissed her deeply, feeling her pour her bright sweetness into him, and he became even more lost in her. Need for her seared him like a white-hot brand. His lips descended to the hollow of her throat. She clung to his shoulders, and he gloried in the way she murmured his name in between sweet, kittenlike sighs.

T.S. felt the sensation of movement, but wasn't aware she had actually moved until her back encountered a solid object. Then she was lifted up onto the deck railing and held tightly, with Logan's arm around her waist.

The tips of her breasts grew taut from his intimate exploration, and she pressed herself deeper into his palm. She cried out when his magic touch glided down her leg and nudged her knees apart. Maddeningly slow, he inched the hem of her dress up to her hips, then burned a pleasure trail along the smooth, bare inner surface of her thighs.

"Is this what you want?" he asked softly, teasing her willing flesh with his fingertips.

"Yes." Her response was as breathy as a sigh. "Please . . . touch me." She kissed his mouth. Their lips parted, then met again in unrestrained passion.

She broke away and moaned softly when his erotic quest ended, and his fingers finally slipped beneath her lace-ledged silk panties and discovered the aching center of her desire. "Don't stop," she said, the utterance a pleasure purr.

Her head fell back, and her eyes drifted closed. Blinding starbursts exploded behind her lids. She rode the crest of each voluptuous sensation. Suddenly, she arched backward in ecstasy—and got the fright of her life.

He reacted the moment he felt her falling by tightening his loose grip around her waist, then swiftly pulled her down to the safety of the solid deck floor. Heart jumping in his chest, he muttered an earthy curse. He realized they were both shaking.

Her shoulders rose and fell with a series of breathy, choking sounds. A stab of guilt buried itself in Logan's chest. "Oh baby, don't cry. It's all right. I've got you. I won't let you go." He pressed a hard kiss on top of her head.

When she raised her face to look at him, he saw laughter, not tears. "I thought you were crying." He grasped her upper arms and shook her slightly. "That little stunt took ten years off my life. You scared the hell out of me!"

Calming down, she gasped out, "Haven't you ever heard of people *falling* in love?"

Gazing helplessly down at her, seeing the amused affection sparkling in her eyes, he regained his sense of humor. "I'd say you almost fell for me."

"Not almost, Logan." Her expression became somber. "I have fallen."

The problems that stood between them rushed back to him. He let go of her. Raking his hand through his hair, he discovered it was unsteady.

Her voice was soft and low as she spoke from her heart. "I can't explain why I feel so strong a bond with you. It's as if you've discovered some special place hidden deep in my soul and set free something so beautiful I can hardly bear it. I don't know what the future may hold for us or if we'll have a future together at all. I only know I want nothing more tonight than to remain in your arms."

Coming from anyone else, Logan would have considered those words embarrassingly insincere. But this was T.S. Sincerity was as much a part of her as her gentle true spirit.

"Loving me may be the biggest mistake you've ever made," he said, knowing that was truer than she could possibly imagine.

His warning gave her a faint tingle of apprehension. Her gaze focused on the sea as she tried to sort out the confused thoughts in her mind. Was she being too reckless in offering herself and her heart with only instinct to guide her? Was he afraid to accept what she was offering for fear of not being able to return her feelings? Or was he simply afraid to trust her because of his own lack of faith in emotions?

She tilted her head slightly and looked searchingly at him. Only Logan and Moon Man had ever aroused such powerful feelings in her. With her first love, she hadn't had the opportunity to explore the depths of those feelings, and perhaps it had been wise not to, given their youth and circumstances. But now, with Logan, T.S. knew she would always regret it if she didn't have the courage to try.

"I am aware of the emotional risks involved," she said. "I'm willing to take my chances, Logan."

His palms grew damp as he returned her direct gaze and imagined he saw his fate written in her serene blue eyes. Fate was something he'd never believed in, but now he wondered if she wasn't an inescapable part of his.

"God help us both," he murmured, digging into his pocket for his keys. Before he could change his mind, he laced his fingers with hers and led her across the deck.

Seconds later, they entered the great room and closed the door behind them.

Turning to her, he leaned down to press a light kiss on her forehead. "Are you sure you know what you're doing?" he asked her gravely.

"I only know I love you," she answered, smiling. "Being with you seems right."

He hesitated, then surprised himself by admitting for the second time that day, "I care about you too." It was only a fraction of the truth. But saying even that much aloud made things more complicated, a voice in the back of his head taunted.

Giving in to his desire for her was madness. How would he ever be able to let her go when the time came?

Recognizing he was still waging some inner battle, T.S. raised a hand to his cheek. "Don't think," she pleaded softly. "Don't try to be logical. Feelings do not have to be logical or justifiable.

128 • THERESA GLADDEN

They simply are what they are. We want each other. Can't we just accept that for now? I'm not asking you for promises you can't make. Please believe that."

Logan swallowed hard, wanting nothing more than to give in to her entreaties. Halfheartedly, he reminded himself it wasn't too late to stop this from happening. But the warmth of her touch, the softening of her cornflower-blue eyes, and the heat of his own desire made him loath to relinquish what they could have together tonight.

"I'm incapable of thinking rationally when I'm with you. T.S., you drive me crazy. You always have." He wrapped his arms around her, drawing her close enough to feel the uncompromising arousal of his body.

She looked up at him through her lashes. "I hope I always will."

His gaze roved over her face for a second before his eyes closed and he lowered his head. His mouth moved across hers slowly, then his lips parted and he thrust his tongue urgently into the soft, warm chamber of her mouth. She welcomed him, matching his demand with a hunger as great as his own.

Logan tumbled blindly into the kiss, powerless to control the way she filled his senses. The fantasy and reality of his past and present desire for her slammed into him. His hands worked frantically, impatiently, sliding up the slender line of her back to her waist, then around until they rested just beneath her breasts.

She groaned, and he drank it in, wondering at the excitement mounting inside him at the simple sound of her expressing her own need. "You feel so good," he murmured against her lips as he gently cupped her small breasts in his hands.

"Please," she gasped, kneading the hard planes of his shoulders.

"Please what? Tell me what you want." He rubbed the tips of his thumbs over her nipples, coaxing forth the sensitive peaks.

She inhaled sharply. "*You!* I want you. Touch me. Hold me." Her hands shook as they moved to his waist and tugged at his shirt.

Hearing her passionate plea and feeling the immediate response of her body, Logan experienced a purely masculine thrill of satisfaction. She was his, he thought with a fierceness that shocked him. She had always been his and always would be—no matter what happened after tonight.

She slipped her hands inside his shirt to explore his bare skin. The sound of the phone ringing mingled with a groan deep in his throat as she trailed her nails across his flat nipples. Caught up in her incredible passion and his surrender to it, he was only distantly aware of the answering machine picking up the call.

He needed her, he thought, anchoring her face between his hands to kiss her again. God, he'd forgotten what it was like to really need, to desperately need, another person. He plunged greedily into her mouth, staking his claim on her completely, intimately.

A mechanical beep was followed by a female voice. "Logan, it's Melissa. If you're there, for God's sake, pick up the phone. Dammit, this is important!"

It took a moment for the urgency in his associate's tone to reach him through the ebb and flow of desire. When it did, he jerked away from T.S. like a guilty teenager caught in the act.

"Listen," he said, holding her at arm's length.

Melissa's voice rose an octave as the message continued. "We're about to lose Neil Spencer! He's been trying to reach you all day, and he's ready to call the whole deal off. Lord, Logan, it's not like you to—"

At the mention of the client's name, Logan's jaw had tightened. He let go of T.S. and rushed into the kitchen to grab the phone. "I'm here. Don't hang up, Melissa. What's going on?"

Sighing with regret over the second interruption of their lovemaking, T.S. walked over to the breakfast bar. She pulled out a chair and sat down to watch as Logan held an agitated conversation with the woman she was sure was the haughty blonde she'd met on her first visit to Hunter Properties.

From his end of the conversation she gathered Logan had been negotiating the sale of some land for a marina and galleria in Duck, a small Outer Banks community north of Nags Head. Apparently, the developer he was working with believed Logan's failure to return his calls that day was an attempt to pull some kind of power play. And, if she was reading the tension seeping into his body accurately, Logan wasn't taking the news very well.

Her lips pursed in a silent whistle when he mentioned the cost of the project at stake. Then her eyes widened with amusement when Logan called Spencer an arrogant, overbearing, paranoid unrepeatable name. Working himself into a frenzy, he ranted at Melissa for her failure to placate the developer. T.S. felt sorry for the poor woman, and hoped she never found herself on the receiving end of one of his tirades. The man certainly knew how to throw a temper tantrum!

After listening as his agent either tried to explain her actions to him or yelled back—T.S. couldn't tell which—he suddenly mumbled an apology, told her he would take care of the situation, and hung up.

"Uh-oh," T.S. said sympathetically. "It sounds like your unscheduled day off caused a bit of trouble."

Logan swung around to face her. She had seen angry men before, but he won the prize. The harsh set of his mouth and the look in his eyes suggested he was well into a state of rage. If his mood ring wasn't red-hot and smoking, she had a feeling it soon would be. She also realized it wasn't going to be easy to pick up where they had left off.

"A bit of trouble?" He strode over to the breakfast bar. "A *bit* of trouble?"

She was proud of herself for not jumping out of her skin when his hands slammed down on the white-tiled surface in front of her. "That's an understatement, huh?" she said with the nervous certainty that he was a volcano about to erupt.

"Do you have any idea who Neil Spencer is?" he asked very slowly, clearly enunciating each word.

She shook her head. "An arrogant, overbearing, paranoid blankety-blank?" Her feeble attempt to lighten the situation was met with a knife-edged stare.

"He's the biggest developer on the East Coast, and a very valuable client." His voice was soft, but it burned the short distance between them. "One I may lose, thanks to you and today's childish little escapade."

She felt her own temper rise in response to his unfair insinuation. Her hands clenched together in her lap as she fought for control. "I'm sure you will be able to resolve the problem when you explain your absence from the office was simply a well-deserved day off and not a power play."

Logan gripped the edge of the breakfast bar, his knuckles whitening. That afternoon, he'd thought he would gladly pay the price for allowing himself to be with her. Never in his blackest imagination would he have thought it would cost him a partnership with one of his most influential clients and more money than the average working stiff ever dreamed of making. The money didn't matter so much, but the loss to his company did. His business was the only thing he'd have when T.S. went away. Work would be the only thing that would keep him sane.

T.S. watched his jaw work back and forth. His angry scowl deepened. "You're not seriously blaming me for what happened, are you?" she asked, hating the quiver in her voice. "I really don't think it was my fault."

"Then whose fault was it?" He retreated to the opposite side of the kitchen as though he couldn't stand being near her any longer. "Who came barging uninvited into my office? If it wasn't for you, I wouldn't have shirked my responsibilities to hang glide off Jockey's Ridge!"

Returning his cold gaze with wide-eyed hurt, she pushed back from the breakfast bar and rose. "I understand you're upset, but that's no excuse for taking your frustration out on me. I know this isn't a good time to ask you to be rational—"

He cut her off. "That's funny. I never had any problem being rational before you came along.

Now I've got a client threatening to pull out of the deal of the century, a runaway kid hiding out on my property, and my finger is turning green from wearing a cheap ring just so you can tell what kind of mood I'm in."

His words struck out at her, but she continued to meet his gaze. Deep in her heart, she knew he didn't mean what he said. Just as she knew he would surely regret it in time. Unfortunately, knowing that didn't lessen the hurt she felt. "I think I should leave now."

"I think that would be best," he said quietly.

"May I have the key to my cottage?"

He searched in his pocket for the key she'd given him when he had picked her up for dinner.

T.S. reached out to catch it when he tossed it to her. She missed and had to bend down to fish it out from under a chair. Straightening, she ordered herself not to cry in front of him.

Silently, she headed for the door. There she stopped and looked over her shoulder. He stood motionless, watching her. She lifted her chin and boldly met his aloof gaze.

"Logan, I admit I behaved impetuously this morning in coming to your office. Sometimes, I think with my heart instead of my brain. I accept responsibility for asking you to spend the day with me. But I didn't *make* you do anything." She saw his detached expression begin to fade. "You made your own decisions. You did what *you* wanted to do. I am sorry for what happened with your client. I hope you will be able to work it out with him."

She waited, giving him a chance to speak. A look of discomfort crossed his face, but he remained silent. She shook her head. "You're a jerk, Logan. But you're a cute jerk."

Continuing to maintain eye contact, she opened the door. Some perverse part of her would not allow her to leave without a reminder of what he had blithely given up tonight. "I want you to know that beneath this boring little black dress, I'm wearing lingerie to die for. Peach silk and sinfully sexy. I bought it yesterday with you in mind. I hope your imagination tortures you all night long."

Having said that, she let herself out and closed the door softly behind her.

Logan's gaze remained fixed upon the space where she had last stood. He had to admire her exit line. T.S. had just taught him another unwanted lesson—even the most gentle of spirits could fight dirty when the need arose—and he wasn't proud of having given her cause to teach it to him.

Moving to the chair she had vacated, he sat down slowly, laboriously. He put his head in his hands, feeling weighed down with self-disgust.

He couldn't believe he'd gone out of his way to hurt her, and in the process hurt himself. Why had he used the incident to drive her away?

He knew the answer to that. If he hadn't, he still wouldn't be suffering anxiety over telling her who he was. The secrets he was keeping from her cast a long shadow over them both. It kept him living in fear of what she would think and feel once she knew.

What kind of person had he become? What had he destroyed in himself years ago when he had run away from being Moon Man Chase? Along with his ability to feel joy and the destruction of his faith in his own emotions, had he also lost the right to love and be loved? Had he given up the right to feel he was a decent human being?

Sighing wearily, he stood up and walked over to the phone. First, he would deal with Spencer. Then he would find T.S. and make amends. He owed her that and so much more. He wished he had the courage to give it all to her.

Eight

T.S. wasn't there when he knocked on her door half an hour later. Noting with relief that her car was still parked beside the cottage, he headed for the one place she could be.

By the bottom step on the beach access, he found her shoes. On impulse he kicked off his own, stripped off his socks, and abandoned them.

Sweeping a searching gaze through the silver twilight, he saw her farther down the strand. She was ambling along the foamy line of surf with her head bent down, arms crossed, hands loosely wrapped around her elbows. The rising moon graced her movements, and the smooth fit of her dress emphasized the sensual quality of her femininity.

As he watched her, he saw her rub her arms lightly, as if to ward off the crisp hint of fall being ushered in by the cooling sea breeze. It wasn't the gesture he unexpectedly found endearing. Another time he might not have noticed it at all. It was her hands looking incredibly small and satiny white against the black fabric of her long, fitted sleeves.

She was a beautiful woman, an intensely feminine one. But her physical self had little to do with the reasons he had loved her sixteen years ago, and had even less influence on his feelings at that moment. His love for her was assured by many things—her alarming frankness, the way she seemed unencumbered by darker complexities of the soul, and the youthful radiance of spirit she had never lost. T.S. Winslow stood for something, something warm, generous, kind, and innocently, if not sometimes foolishly, courageous.

Logan started toward her. As his feet stirred up the soft sand and left grainy showers in his wake, he was assailed with a strange kind of suffering. It was the perverse sense of the unearned joy brought by her loving him. If he lived a thousand lifetimes, it was a debt he could never discharge.

T.S. didn't hear him approaching over the constant drone of the wind and roar of the ocean. It was only by chance she happened to glance up and see him advancing toward her. Something about the way he moved with an energetic, restless stride sent up a flare of memory. But it was quickly replaced by the rising tide of her emotions.

Her pulse quickened, not in surprise but in anticipation. Somehow she had known he would eventually come looking for her. She hadn't expected it would be so soon.

She stopped to wait for him.

He came to a halt in front of her. "Would you like to know what color my mood ring is?"

"Sexually frustrated, I hope?" she drawled lightly. The wind feathered through his dark blond hair.

Her eyes followed the movement of his hand as he pushed a lock back from his forehead.

A brief grin softened the harsh line of his mouth. "Contrite . . . *and* frustrated, T.S. I owe you an apology. I knew I was acting like a jerk, but couldn't seem to stop. It wasn't fair to blame you for what happened."

"You hurt me." Her artless statement of fact without censure was accompanied by a direct, unblinking stare.

A shadow of pain passed over his features, as fleeting as twilight. He nodded, accepting his due measure of guilt. "I know. And I'd rather cut out my heart than ever hurt you again. I'm sorry. Will you forgive me for being such a jerk?"

"I already have. I knew you were really angry at yourself and not at me."

Sighing, she continued her slow stroll through the surf, which pooled and receded over her bare feet. Her hands betrayed her unusual state of nervous tension as she tightly gripped her forearms.

He fell into step beside her. His solid presence silently accompanying her along the windswept shore filled her senses. She had to subdue those senses and force her mind to focus on the thoughts and questions that had troubled her before his arrival.

"What hurt me tonight was the way you used the incident with your client," she said suddenly, drawing his gaze to her profile. "I think it gave you an excuse to back away from what was happening between us."

"You're right." He drew in a long, uneven breath. "I got scared."

She stopped in midstride and stared at him,

then turned her back on him. "Have I—" She broke off, hearing the odd catch in her voice. Shakily, she began again. "It's the strangest thing, but I feel like I've known you forever. I keep forgetting we've only known each other less than a week."

Logan's eyes clouded. Mixed feelings winged through him. "Instant affinity," he murmured.

"Yes, you could call it that." She sighed. "Anyway, I guess I've tried to rush things. It's part of my impetuous nature. When something feels right, I steamroller ahead, wanting whatever I want, wanting it yesterday, so to speak. That method works when I've set my sights on some-*thing*, but it doesn't necessarily work with people." She gripped her hands tightly together. "Have I repelled you by coming on too strong? Maybe you think I do this sort of thing all the time. Chase men, I mean."

He put his arms around her waist. "T.S.—"

"No. Let me finish what I have to say." She broke free and moved a few steps farther into the water, keeping her back to him. "I've even considered that you might think I'm trying to use sex to influence you to sell the Greensboro property. I swear, Logan, neither of those things is true. I don't use sex as a bargaining tool, and I don't chase after men. With you I've found myself in a unique situation."

She turned to face him. "Is it so difficult for you to trust me when I say I love you?"

The distress Logan saw in her eyes filled him with guilt and remorse in a way her words never could. An errant memory came back to him of her sitting alone in a bus station, looking lost, confused, and as able to fend for herself as a newborn

...mb. Her eyes had held the same hint of distress, ... haunting sadness. Past and present, her emotions affected him more powerfully than his own.

He stepped closer and reached out to catch her wrist. Her whole body tensed, he noticed with regret. "Nothing you have said or done has been the least repellent to me."

Unable to maintain eye contact with him, she lowered her head. He raised her hand and lightly touched his lips to her palm. In response, she felt heat rushing over her skin.

"Look at me," he demanded softly. With a curved finger, he stroked the underside of her chin, then tilted her head back until she met his gaze. "That's better. I've never thought you were using sex to influence me to sell the property. I don't do business in bed, and I know you don't either. In fact, I'd punch out anyone who dared insinuate that you do." A smile tipped the corners of his mouth. "So watch what you say." He touched his fist to her jaw in a fake right hook and was pleased by her brief smile.

His expression grew serious. "T.S., I've never questioned your integrity or sincerity." He stroked his thumb along her cheek. "You wear your integrity and sincerity on your beautiful face."

Her heart squeezed in her chest. "Then what's wrong, Logan?" she asked softly. "What have I done to make you run from me?"

He withdrew his hand from her face. "You haven't done anything. It's me. Running is what I do best." His voice was heavy with strain as he acknowledged he had even more in common with the boy hiding in the storage room on his property. After all these years he was still running, and hiding too. "I started running years ago, and I just realized I never stopped. I've been running from myself, from what feel for you."

His admission left T.S. speechless as she tried to comprehend what she was hearing. Something in his past must have hurt him deeply for him to go to such an extreme. She hated whatever or whoever had robbed him of his laughter and made him feel the need to hide behind a wall of fire.

Hesitantly, she said, "Do you want to talk about it? I won't try to offer solutions or make judgments. I'll just listen."

His eyes widened as he looked at her. In them she saw longing and—to her shock—fear.

"No." He shook his head. "I don't want to talk about it right now." His gaze strayed to the open sea, then back to her. "But I will tell you this much. I'm tired of running, of pretending I don't need anything or anyone. I do need you. I need your laughter and bright colors. Your honesty. The generosity of your spirit."

"Oh, Logan, I need you too."

He lightly rested his hand upon her cheek. His gaze traveled from her lips to the crescent-moon and stars medallion, then to the gentle swell of her hips. When his eyes returned to hers, they were blazing with intensity. "I don't have the right to ask—and God knows, I don't deserve it—but I want to make love with you, and sleep with you curled against my body, your heart beating beneath my hand. I want to kiss you awake in the morning and make love to you all over again. Will you come home with me now?"

Her heart beat furiously in response to his arousing plea and his naked display of emotion. The depth of his feelings, the shock and thrill over the tentative step he'd taken beyond his defensive wall of fire, blurred her vision with the threat of tears.

The only thing he hadn't said were the three words she wished with all her heart to hear. She knew she couldn't expect too much from him too soon, though. In time, perhaps, she told herself hopefully.

She swayed toward him and lifted her hands to his face. "I love you," she whispered fiercely. Rising up on her toes, she pressed her lips to his.

He dragged her against him. His tongue swept deeply into her mouth, seeking her own in an intimate duel. The sweet liquid of her passion communicated itself to him and all but blinded him with need. He moved his trembling hands over her face, through her wind-kissed curls, along the slender length of her body, down to the softness of her thighs pressing against the hardness of his own.

Once again, he found himself only seconds away from stripping the clothing from her body and laying her down on the wet sand.

"T.S." His breath teased the sensitive inner fold of her ear. "What color did you say your lingerie was?"

He felt her smile against the hollow of his cheek. "Let's go home, and I'll show you."

As they walked toward his beachfront house, the Atlantic Ocean rose and fell against the beach, and above in the darkening sky the stars, which had not been visible earlier, twinkled merrily as though they were aware of all that had happened and were highly amused.

Logan knew there were many things he could, and should, say to her. Leaving the strand behind, he wished he could tell her he loved her. But those

words stuck in his throat. Saying them wou[...]
make him feel stripped bare as driftwood.

Climbing the stairs to his house, he struggled to
find a way to reveal his identity to her. But his
courage balked at blurting out, *Oh, by the way,
remember that kid who rescued you in a bus station sixteen years ago? The one you think sold you
back to your father? Guess what, I used to be a
skinny, long-haired hippie kid named Moon Man.*
After all that had happened tonight, he didn't
believe either of them could bear the shock of his
confession and still remain together to welcome
the morning light.

Entering the house, Logan heedlessly shoved all
thoughts aside except for one. She was his now.
That was all that mattered. He told himself problems could be worked out tomorrow when he
wasn't so caught up in desire, fighting to break
free.

Switching on a lamp in the great room, he stood
gazing at her. For the second time in his life he
said a silent prayer. If it was answered, come
morning she would be so strongly bonded to him,
Logan Hunter, not even the sins of the past would
separate them.

He went to her, took her hand, and led her to the
threshold of his bedroom. There, he could wait no
longer to fold her into his embrace. His mouth
came down over hers, hard and hungry for the
taste of her.

T.S. responded with unchecked passion. She
tightened her grip on his arms, loving the solid feel
of his body against hers. She felt as if heat waves
of desire and something deeper, more indefinable,
were pouring out of him and into her.

He raised his head and gazed at her with unarded arousal and need. "I can barely breathe from wanting you," he whispered hoarsely.

Dazed, she rested her forehead on his chest. "Until you opened the door and I fell into your arms the night we met, I didn't know I'd been waiting for you."

"T.S." He rocked her from side to side, pressing kisses over her hair. A groan of pleasure escaped him, and he closed his eyes.

With shaking hands she pulled at the shirt tucked into his pants. His hands joined hers in frantic movements until together they got his shirt off and dumped it on the floor.

"So soft and silky," she murmured, spreading her fingers through the curling mass on his chest. She found one of his nipples with the tip of her tongue.

Her caress made him suck in his breath. "Stop." He stepped back, catching her hands and holding them captive.

"You didn't like that?" she asked in concern.

"I like it too much. If you don't want to be thrown down on the floor and ravished—"

Her laughter interrupted him. "I've never been ravished on the floor. I think I would adore it."

He shook his head. "I've got other plans for you and your sinfully sexy underwear."

She smiled wickedly. "I take it my grand exit line got to you, huh?"

He locked his arms around her waist, lifted her off her feet, and started walking. "You know it did, you witchy woman. It's show-and-tell time."

Laughing, she wrapped her arms around his neck as he carried her through the dark room. When he sat her down on his king-sized bed, she tried to pull him down with her, but he resisted.

"Not yet," he whispered against her lips as he gently pried her hands from his neck. "Don't move, sweet T.S. Don't take your clothes off, because I want to do that. Be back in a moment."

Feeling impatient and ridiculously nervous, she watched his shadowy form travel to the window. He opened the drapes, letting in the light of the full moon nestled within the blue-black heaven.

When he disappeared into the adjoining bathroom, she removed her earrings and laid them on the nightstand. She leaned back on her elbows and closed her eyes. Wishing he would hurry back, she listened to cabinets being opened and closed, water running.

Seconds later, she opened her eyes, and her pulse began pounding. In the doorway between the two rooms, Logan stood rakishly at ease, wearing only charcoal trousers, one upraised hand resting on the doorjamb. His other hand lay negligently against his thigh, fingers loosely clasping a towel. Ghostly silver moonlight smoothed over his broad shoulders and down the inviting musculature of his chest.

Something in his stance and his expression made him look dangerous and exciting at the same time. A tiny shiver of recognition went through her. Moon Man used to look like that to her. Oh God, she thought. Even as she wanted Logan with a passion almost too hot to bear, she could not help feeling regret for what might have been with the love of her youth. She locked that last thought away in her heart.

She watched the man she loved walk at an unhurried pace toward her. Her smile was brilliant and unknowingly arousing.

"If a million women smiled at me," he said, "not

one of their smiles would have the effect of yours."
His voice stroked her like velvet.

The blood flowing through her veins heated to a
blistering intensity. If possible, her smile grew
brighter. "How does it affect you?"

He traced one corner of her mouth with a
fingertip. "It brings light to the dark places. You
make me happy. Remember that. Promise you'll
remember that no matter what happens."

"I promise. You make me happy too." Before she
could do more than fleetingly wonder about his
dark places, he was kneeling on the floor, running his hands down her legs, which dangled over
the side of the bed. She jerked in reflex when he
picked up her bare right foot. "Logan? What are
you—"

"Lie still," he said, stopping her attempt to rise
by placing his other hand on the curve of her hip.

"But I want to touch you. I want—"

"I know. You'll have your chance. This is just
the beginning. Let me take care of you first."

She sighed as she submitted. Slowly, he set
about washing away all traces of sand and dried
sea salt from her feet and legs.

Afterward, taking each foot in turn, he lavishly
explored every inch from toes to ankle with his
mouth and tongue. Small, breathy sounds welled
up in her throat as beguiling, almost unbearable,
sensations shivered up to the lower region of her
body. Never in her wildest imagining would she
have thought the washing and kissing of feet
could be so . . . *so sexual.*

His fingers slipped upward, lightly massaging
the taut sinews of her legs. Her heart skipped a
beat or two, and the tightness in her throat spread
to the tips of her breasts. His clever fingers and his

warm, moist mouth worked their way to her thighs, bringing every nerve vividly alive.

She abandoned herself to his touch, to the steadily increasing pressure within her body, losing herself in him as he lost himself in the joy of loving her. Her thoughts seemed to twist and circle into themselves like an intricate design worked in tapestry. Passion wrapped languorous chains around her mind until thinking became as difficult as sawing through steel with an emery board. Her eyes blinked open suddenly when she felt his warm breath vibrate against the silk fabric covering the delta of her parted thighs. She realized her dress was pushed up past her hips and wondered how that had happened. His intimate exploration made her dizzy with need. She heard a softly pleading voice, and it took her a second to recognize it as her own. Arching her body, she called his name in an anguished cry of desire.

She reached for him at the same time he wrapped his arms around her waist and lifted her off the bed. For a long moment, he held her against him, stroking her skin to a feverish pitch. She turned her head weakly and pressed her lips to the heavily beating pulse in his throat.

"Logan, please. Kiss me." The words came out in a rush. Her lips ached to be touched and caressed. But he only bent his head to rub his mouth back and forth over the translucent skin above her collarbone.

Logan wove his fingers through her windswept curls and tilted her head back to look at her. A beautiful passion flush had spread over her cheeks, and her eyes had a radiance that was almost liquid. He could feel the needy tension in his body relax into something tender and worshipful. His mouth covered hers in a long, deep kiss.

Still in possession of her mouth, he eased her down the length of him until her feet touched the thick pile carpet. He said her name once, and it sounded like a whispered prayer from his kiss-swollen lips to hers.

Raising his head, he smiled down at her. She answered him with a slow, delicious, delighted smile of her own. Forcing air into his lungs, he reached for the hem of her dress and pulled it up. She lifted her arms and helped him remove it.

He leaned back, giving her a slow, sensual appraisal. "You were right. Peach silk and sinfully sexy. Designed to inflame the desire of the man who has the good fortune of removing it from the body of the woman wearing it."

"Are you inflamed?" she asked in a quiet, interested voice as she floated the tips of her fingers across the downy soft hair on his chest.

"Burning hotter with each passing second." With one finger he traced shifting sensual patterns along the swell of her breasts, then moved on to circle the outline of her nipples through the pale silk. He took almost as much delight in her sharply indrawn breath as he did the heat exploding within his own body.

His heated gazed locked on the medallion lying between her breasts. *Love endures.* It hadn't just endured, he thought. It had grown stronger, so strong it filled every fiber of his being. He bent to kiss the place where the crescent moon and stars touched her skin.

Wanting, needing, more, T.S. reached around her back and began unhooking the bustier. Small, seductive sounds hummed in her throat as she struggled out of the garment. "Logan." She lifted her hands to his face, communicating her desire in each caress. "Make love to me."

Groaning, he buried his face in her hair and slid his hands down to cup and stroke her breasts. The wildly primitive urges flowing through him stunned and fascinated him. He branded kisses along her shoulder, across the ivory swell of her breasts and their straining dusty-rose tips.

She was everything he had ever imagined she would be. Everything he'd ever wanted. All compelling heat, yielding, demanding, as smooth to the touch as the silk panties she wore, and so maddeningly fragrant. Delicate as spring flowers. Heady wine simmered with spices. He brought his mouth back to hers in a fast, fervent kiss that left them both reeling and rocky.

Impatiently, she unbuckled his belt and tossed it aside, then pulled at his trousers. With his frenzied assistance they were both stripped bare and tumbling back onto the bed.

They lay flesh upon flesh. Their movements became wild with the need to explore new textures and new flavors. Together they pushed closer and closer to the edge of reason.

Logan dragged them both up onto their knees. For a moment he simply held her tightly against him, feeling as though he could draw her inside himself. Running his hand down her arm, he took her hand and carried it to his hardened masculinity. "I need your touch," he whispered, his breath feathering across her brow like a butterfly's kiss. He closed his eyes, becoming mindlessly lost in the magic her small hand worked upon his aching, throbbing body.

Words of need filled him and spilled out in a

frantic torrent. "So right. It feels so right to have you in my arms. You fill my home and my life with your bright colors. T.S., you make me feel complete."

"I love you," she whispered over and over as she sank down onto the bed with him. His body flowed over hers, enveloping her with his power and intensity. She wrapped her legs around his hips in a silent, urgent appeal.

He felt her straining against him, whimpering, "Please, love, please . . ." Looking down, he saw her eyes darken with arousal and a rose-tinted flush of love-desire stain her ivory complexion. Breathing became difficult as her hands slid over his thighs. Fighting to conquer the urgent demands of his own desire, he forced himself to say, "Not yet, sweetheart. I have to protect you."

She gave him a martyr's look of frustration, but she freed him from the embrace of her legs and arms. "Be quick about it, my love. Wrap that rascal. I'm dying. Here, let me help you," she said, eagerly sitting up.

He laughed as he gently pushed her back down. "Don't you dare try to *help* me," he said, leaning across the bed to search the drawer of the nightstand. "If you do, I'm afraid we won't need it anymore. I'm ready to go off like skyrockets on the Fourth of July as it is."

He was still chuckling when he came back to her, prepared and ready to take them both to the limits of their shared passion. His lips descended to her throat in a hungry caress before his mouth covered hers. The way she rose up to meet his kiss and opened herself to the exploration of his fingers saturated his senses. The very air he breathed became thicker than warm clover honey.

He stroked her lips with his while he painted the impression of the feel of her body into his mind to keep and hold forever. His fingers found the warm, damp inner petals of her femininity. He smoothed, courted, caressed, every satin inch until he felt her shiver uncontrollably.

"Now, T.S. I need you now," he whispered. "By morning I want your soul so tangled up with mine, neither of us will ever be free of the other."

"Make me happy, Logan," she whispered back, loving his face with her hands. She closed her eyes, gasping at the sweetness of his flesh pressing against the heart of her desire.

"Let's make each other happy." He slowly buried himself inside her.

Blindly, she slid her legs around his waist. T.S. knew nothing beyond the exquisite fit of their bodies, hot ecstasy, and the miracle of love taking place. She could feel the cadence of their hearts in unison as they fell into a rhythm so perfectly matched, they might have always been together.

Logan's fingers curled around her writhing hips, and he lifted himself to gaze down into her face. Jubilant emotions shimmered over her delicate features, and the fierce sweetness of her possessed him totally. Love whispered through him for the woman answering his motions, quivering with deep satisfaction each time he thrust into her. Feeling her body shudder on the crest of rapture, he took her face between his hands and kissed her deeply. Love and tenderness twisted his heart. Did it show in his eyes, his smile, his face?

"I love you," she repeated, her voice a low, pure melody.

Their eyes met, a slow joining of spirit to spirit. He watched the pattern of her breathing change and her lips form a smile. The radiance of that smile brought him to a towering peak, and he filled her with his love.

Minutes later, when they could move again, they got up to turn back the bed linen, all the while touching, laughing, and teasing. Lying down with him once more, T.S. snuggled her back against him. She smiled sleepily as he placed one hand over her breast.

With the steady beat of her heart beneath his palm, Logan buried his face in her silky hair and closed his eyes.

Sometime during the night, he woke from a dream filled with hot, voluptuous sensations. He raised up on one elbow and gazed down at T.S. She looked like a ravished angel with red-gold curls for a halo. She lay on her back, one small hand curled against her cheek, a sated smile parting her lips.

Just looking at her filled him with fragile emotion and raging lust. Smiling at her, he allowed his thoughts to drift like the sweetest of fantasies to another time, to a hot summer night in another place with the girl this woman had been. . . .

Moon Man lay awake on the sofa, head pillowed on his hands. It was too hot to sleep, and the hazy fluorescence of street lamps shone directly into Jack's tiny apartment. Traffic sounds came in through the open window, and noises of adults at play seeped through the cracks in the floor—

laughter, music, voices raised both in conversation and in an occasional drunken brawl.

A longing for the peacefulness of home and cool mountain breezes created a hollow ache inside him. Shifting restlessly, he firmly told himself he'd get used to the city. But he doubted he'd ever get used to sleeping in his jeans the way he had for the past three nights.

A soft, mewing cry drew his gaze to the sleeping princess across the room. His ears had become sharply attuned to that heartbreaking little sound. It signaled the onset of bad dreams that visited her every night, but to his amazement, never woke her.

Getting up, he silently padded over to the single bed and stared down at her.

T.S. looked so beautiful with her titian hair streaming over the pillow. The white sheet pooled at her waist and clung to her slender hips. Her lips were slightly parted, one hand curled against her cheek. Tears glistened like liquid gemstones upon the thick lashes of her closed eyes. With every shallow, breathy sob she took, he could see the swell and fall of her breasts beneath the tie-dyed shirt she wore.

And as he had every night, he felt her loneliness and confusion as keenly as his own. He gently placed his trembling hand on her shoulder. "It's all right, love. I'm with you. Please don't cry." With the tips of his fingers, he caught the moisture seeping from the corners of her eyes. Stroking her hair, he murmured words he could never say to her in the light of day.

Suddenly, the tears ceased to flow, and she quieted. It was as if the soft assurance in his voice and the tenderness of his touch reached into her nightmares and chased them away. It happened every time he comforted her in the night. He shook his head in wonder over the strange little miracle.

Yearning built up inside him. His lower body hardened, and he fought against it. Slowly, reluctantly, he untangled his fingers from the silken web of her hair.

He sank to his knees. Careful not to disturb her, he folded his arms on the edge of the narrow bed and lowered his chin to rest on his wrists. Wishing for impossible things, he watched while his princess slept.

"Logan?"

The soft whisper pulled him back from the past. Yet even as his thoughts returned to the present, he became frighteningly aware of something having happened inside him. His two separate worlds had collided with the impact of a star going nova. The broken halves of him—the boy he had been and the man he had become—irrevocably fused into one.

For a moment he was frozen by a fear of the unknown. He wasn't Moon Man Chase. He wasn't Logan Hunter. It was as if the two had joined in some inexplicable way, forming a new and as yet undefined being. His heart began trying to hammer its way through bone, muscle, and skin. The enormity of it, the incomprehension, stunned him.

Then a soft, small hand reached through his internal chaos and lovingly touched his face. His fear faded into acceptance. His heartbeat returned to normal. A peace like none he'd ever known descended upon him. For the first time in his adult life, he felt whole.

"Yes, sweetheart, I'm with you," he murmured, gathering her into his arms.

She sought his mouth in a lingering kiss full of desire and promise. Rolling over to capture his body beneath hers, she eased him into her warmth.

The once-emotional renegade savored every emotion that winged through his spirit. Slowly, easily, gloriously, he stayed with her body and soul until they reached the place where stars are born and heaven beats within the human heart.

Long after the loving, Logan remained awake and kept watch over the sleeping princess who had unknowingly brought the sweetest of all miracles into his life.

Nine

Dawn sent slivers of pink-streaked daylight to chase away the lingering shadows. T.S. awakened to the pleasurable sensation of Logan's warm body tangled with hers, his arm a sweet pressure on her midriff, his palm curved beneath the pliable mound of her breast.

Opening her eyes, she looked around in a softly unfocused way and saw dust motes swimming in a sunbeam above her head. For a moment she lay still, savoring the joy of waking up beside Logan, listening to the muted roar of the morning tide and the call of gulls circling in the sky outside the window.

She stretched like a cat in total, lazy satisfaction, feeling the trifling soreness in the more delicate parts of her body. A happy, cherished sensation welled up inside her as a delightful sweep of last night's memories came back to her.

Being alive and in love was wonderful. Someone ought to tell the rest of the world, she thought, snuggling deeper against Logan. It should be bottled and sold as a wonder drug, a cure-all, the highest of all highs. She bit her lower lip to keep from laughing out loud over her incredibly love-dazed thoughts.

She felt a faint movement as Logan stirred, then rolled away, depriving her of his warmth and touch. She twisted onto her side and studied the man who possessed her heart so thoroughly. Sleep softened his granite features so that they were rather boy-ishly vulnerable. Dawn's soft light tickled his thick lashes and played in his rakishly tousled hair, picking out the finest strands of gold. The white linen sheet twisted and foamed like sea froth around his magnificently sprawled body.

Her heart contracted as she watched him in his unguarded state of slumber. Although her body and mind still held the flavors, impressions, and sheer wonder of his lovemaking, she greedily wanted more. On the beach, the night before, he had said he wanted to kiss her awake in the morning and make love to her all over again. Well, morning was here, she was too alert and burning with passion to go back to sleep, and he was out colder than a KO'd boxer.

T.S. sighed. As much as she disliked robbing him of the privilege he had requested, something had to be done. If she could just get him started on the trip back to the land of awareness, she could *pretend* to be asleep. She nudged his foot with hers. She rubbed her toes up his ankle to his knee and back again. *Nothing.*

Desperate times, she told herself, called for despicable sneakiness. She sat up and carefully inched the sheet back a little. Leaning over him, she blew lightly on his belly button. Beyond the contraction of his stomach muscles, nothing happened. A waste of hot air. She tried tickling his ribs and made a little progress. He wiggled provocatively, and the bed linen dipped enticingly lower on his hips. Another tickle rolled him onto his side, displaying to her appreciative eyes a tush to die for.

Yes, indeed. Things were looking up. She worked nibbling kisses along his spine. He made a purring sound in his throat and turned over onto his stomach. Hang it all, she fumed impatiently, just how exhausted could a man be after a night of mad, passionate love?

Brows drawing together in a frown, she lowered herself onto one elbow. Starting at the curve of his buttocks, her gaze followed the pleasure trip her hand took up the valley of his back.

Suddenly, T.S. stiffened. She jerked her hand away as if the heat of his body burned her.

Her gaze riveted to the place where her palm had been. High on his right shoulder blade was an intriguing birthmark. A strawberry moon. A crescent moon.

So that's how he got his name. The words of a long-ago thought echoed in her head. She could see her younger self, eyes shining, experiencing her fist sensations of physical desire as she stared at the naked back of a heroic golden-haired boy.

"Moon Man," she whispered, reaching out to touch the moon with a trembling fingertip. A soft smile of reverent wonder slowly spread across her mouth.

Confusion cascaded through her, and her smile quickly faded. She let her hand fall to her side again. Oh God, it wasn't possible! Logan Hunter could not be Moon Man. It was just another coincidence. An illusion. A strange quirk of fate. Yet, even while her mind desperately denied what she was seeing and thinking, her heart acknowledged the truth.

Disoriented thoughts revolved like a rapidly spinning roulette wheel in her head.

"What do I know about Logan Hunter? His professional life is an open book. On a personal level he's a mystery. My impression, though, is that he's a straight arrow. . . ."

Hard eyes and a mouth that looked like it had to work hard for a smile . . .

The past isn't important. . . .

Princess . . .

If you don't like the world you're pushed into, you go out and create a new one. . . .

Eyes wide with the shock of her discovery, T.S. eased off the bed. For a moment she stared numbly at him. Her heart began to pound, and her body shook as she no longer had the comfort of denial. The evidence was undeniable. "Logan is Moon Man," she whispered in a tortured voice.

A sick feeling rose from her stomach to her throat. Covering her mouth with one hand, she fled into the bathroom and quietly closed the door behind her.

Seconds later, she was on her knees, emptying the contents of her stomach until there was nothing left but dry heaves and an unbearable pressure in her chest. When the dry heaves subsided, she flushed the toilet and lowered the lid. She cradled her face in her hand. Her body ached as though she had the flu.

Rising on shaky legs, she turned on the tap water, rinsed her mouth, then used his toothbrush. She grabbed a hand towel, soaked it, and roughly applied it to her face, then threw it in the sink. Gripping the edge of the Carrera marble countertop, she glanced in the mirror and hardly recognized the wild-eyed, ashen-faced woman staring back.

She lifted one badly trembling hand and closed her fingers in a vise grip around the medallion she'd worn as a symbol of comfort, hope, and enduring love for so many years. Pain slammed into her again, almost bringing her to her knees. Bitterly, she let her hand fall back down to the marble counter as she forced herself to remain upright.

All at once, T.S. pulled herself together. What had been helpless shock and denial abruptly flared into anger, an anger so furious it burned her eyes like a living flame.

Last night while she'd repeatedly told him she loved him, not only with words but with her body, he'd continued to run from himself, run from his past—a past he had once shared with her! All through the exquisite wonder of their lovemaking, he had known who she was, and he had kept his secrets from her.

Once, Moon Man had lied to her and betrayed her. Long ago, she had forgiven him because he had protected, comforted, listened to, fed, and sheltered her, asking nothing in return. Now this man he had become, this Logan Hunter, had betrayed her again by remaining cruelly silent. He had taken her love and used it. He had withheld his secrets, withheld his trust.

Humiliation and rage mounted inside her. She opened the door and strode into the bedroom. Her angry gaze locked on the man on the bed. He was still asleep, looking even more vulnerable than before, curled up on his side, hugging a pillow. The faint desire to kiss his brow and smooth back the lock of hair falling across his forehead came without warning. She hardened her heart against such softer feelings, telling herself she didn't want to kiss him, she wanted to kill him, to hurt him as he had hurt her past and present.

She blew a breath out slowly and walked over to the bed. Snatching the pillow from his arms, she hit him on the head with it. "Wake up," she said loudly, sharply. She struck a blow on his shoulder. "I said wake up, dammit!"

"T.S., what are you trying to do?" He jackknifed up.

"I'm trying to kill Logan Hunter or Moon Man Chase or whatever you call yourself," she shouted, hitting him repeatedly. "Liar. Cheating, deceiving liar." Tears blinded her vision, choked her voice.

He knocked the pillow away. Losing control, she continued to hurl vindictive words at him as she struck out with her hand. He blocked the blow with his forearm.

She barely had time to assimilate what was happening as he seized both her wrists in an aggressive grip. Deep sobs racked her insides as she struggled violently, trying to fight free. With a savage yank she was jerked off her feet. She fell across Logan. Then he was rolling her over and pinning her to the mattress with his body.

White-hot rage poured out of her along with tears as she kept fighting, calling on every ounce of bitterness and hurt trapped inside her heart. She writhed and twisted and tried to kick at his legs. Working her hands loose, she pulled at his hair. He caught her flailing hands again and anchored them over her head.

"It's okay, calm down. Stop it, T.S.," he said softly over and over, but she was beyond hearing. Finally, she exhausted herself with useless struggles. Damp with perspiration, she lay still beneath him, breathing in great shuddering gasps.

Frantically, she tried to corral her senses and regain control over them. A part of her registered her success as her tears ceased abruptly. But she was aware of the last trickle sliding down her cheek to hang suspended on her earlobe, just as she was aware of Logan's weight and his hard, hair-roughened legs lying along the inside of her thighs.

Logan let go of her hands. He threaded his fingers through her wildly disordered curls and brushed his mouth over her temple, fearing it would be the last time she would allow him the right. Raising his head, he anxiously searched her face. The eyes that had looked at him with hero worship, the eyes that had looked at him with love, were aswim with pain that burned him to the soul, and he hated the part of him that had caused her that pain.

"So, you know," he said quietly, controlling his voice with great effort.

"Yes, I know."

As she turned her head to one side and shut her eyes tight, rejection sliced through him like a sharp, angry blade. "I wanted to tell you last night on the beach, but I just couldn't find the words."

"You should have tried harder."

"Yes, I should have. I'm sorry."

"I don't care if you're sorry. You've known all along who I am. But I didn't—" She broke off. There was accusation enough in that statement. She didn't need to go on.

"I knew that first night. I recognized you before you even told me your name. Do you want to know what I felt?"

"No."

The dull, lifeless tone of her voice sent panic racing along Logan's nerve endings. He had to make her listen, had to make her understand. "Too bad, because I'm going to tell you anyway," he said, forcing himself to speak calmly. "At first I was scared to death you would recognize me, and if you did, I knew I couldn't lie to myself about who I was anymore." He stopped and dragged in a shaky breath. Was she even listening? he wondered. Had she retreated somewhere in her mind where she couldn't hear or feel him?

His fingers worked convulsively in her silken hair. He knew he could easily turn her head, forcing her to look at him and acknowledge what he was saying, but he wanted her to meet his eyes of her own accord. "Look at me, T.S.," he begged softly. "I want you to look into my eyes so you can see that everything I'm about to tell you is true. *Look* at me."

T.S. slowly turned her head, aware of the slight expansion of her chest that came with each shaken inhalation, aware of Logan's body tensing above hers. Her gaze found and held his. In his eyes she saw a reflection of her own grief and pain, the helplessness that came when even the strongest human beings were faced with their own terrible fragility.

Fear curled in Logan's stomach. He was losing her. "T.S., please—" He stopped as he heard the desperation in those two words.

She sensed his need for her to listen, to forgive, to comfort, and within herself she felt an over-whelming urge to weep and fulfill his needs. How often, she asked herself, had she done that for others while ignoring her own needs? Far too often, came the answer. This time her hurt, her grief, her inability to cope were too great to willingly let go of. "Get off me," she said in a dead-flat voice. "Then maybe I'll listen."

He stared at her, then abruptly rolled over, releasing her from the prison of his body. She watched him sit up, bracing his back against the headboard, his knees slightly flexed.

Tension was visible across his shoulders and his face, giving the impression of something powerful trying to emerge. When he spoke, his voice was rough, not quite under control. "My dad was an idealist, a dreamer, who got disillusioned with the Haight-Ashbury scene. So he founded a commune he called Freedom Farm on some land he inherited in the mountains of West Virginia. Sean—that's my dad, I called him Sean—was this great big bear of a man with shaggy blond hair and a beard, and John Lennon wire-rimmed glasses. He loved freedom, the beauty of nature, and giving authority a black eye and the finger." He laughed softly in remembrance of things only he could see behind his closed eyes.

"My mom, Summer, grew every kind of flower and spice imaginable," he continued with indulgent affection. "She spun wool from the sheep we raised and dyed it and wove her own cloth. She was the original earth mother, wanting to take care of everyone who came within her orbit." He paused. "You remind me of her, wanting everyone to be happy and cared for."

He glanced at T.S. through layers of memories and emotions. He saw she had sat up and gathered the sheet around her as though her nakedness embarrassed her. The simple gesture made him feel incredibly sad. He wanted to touch and hold her, but he forced himself to keep still. "Sounds nice, doesn't it?"

"Yes, it does." T.S. knew there was a snake somewhere in the idyllic picture he painted of his parents and Freedom Farm, but she didn't know when and where it would strike.

His brows drew together in a seething scowl. "I didn't know I was different until I went to school. Then I was made to feel different, *bad* different. When we met in that bus station, I think I was the angriest person on the face of this earth. I was angry because I didn't want to be a hippie kid in a normal world, angry because I had been laughed at and hated for being strange when I wanted to be the same as everybody else. I just couldn't take being who I was anymore."

"I don't understand." T.S. shook her head. Her diffused anger was rapidly changing into an aching misery. She sighed. "What was so terrible about being who you were?"

He blew out a hard breath as he turned his face to stare out the window. Mentally, he examined the jagged scars he carried inside. "Do you remember your first day of school, T.S.? I'll never forget mine. I was nervous and excited. I desperately wanted to be liked and accepted. When my parents took me into the classroom, the whole place got quiet. So quiet I could hear my own heart beating. The teacher looked at us with this pinched, angry expression on her face. The kids stared, stared at our odd homemade clothes, stared at my long hair, stared at the love beads my father wore. Then the snickers and whispering started. From that day on, those kids made my life hell. They called me a dirty hippie. Made fun of the way I dressed, spoke, and acted. They talked about television shows I'd never seen, games I'd never played. I talked about going to Washington, D.C., for peace marches and parroted my family's political views. They talked about their brothers and sisters. I talked about the Rainbow Woman, the Music Maker, and other people who lived on the commune. We didn't speak the same language."

He paused, feeling the hurt and anger of the child hidden deep inside him. It tore him apart to know that after so many years, he couldn't speak about his childhood without his stomach clenching and his throat constricting. "I didn't know until years later that the teacher's son had died in Vietnam and my father's conscientious objector status had been an obscenity to her. Her hatred extended to me, and she let me know it in the most subtle ways."

"How?" T.S. asked in a hoarse whisper.

Logan reluctantly looked at her. Tears shimmered in her eyes, and behind them an anger as bright as his own. He curled his hand into a fist to keep from reaching out to her. "By pretending not to notice when a kid tripped me when she called me up to the board, and by giving silent approval to cruel taunts and jeers. Every time I made a mistake, she would say pointedly, 'Now, children, remember Moon Man is different from us. He wasn't raised in a normal, decent Christian home. He just doesn't know any better. We'll have to teach him the *right* way to do things, won't we?'"

"How awful," T.S. said, her voice filled with compassion as she momentarily forgot her own grievances against him.

Logan shrugged impatiently. He didn't want her pity. He just wanted her understanding. "After that, the differences between me and the rest of the world just kept becoming more and more apparent. That summer after school was out, my father took me with him to pick up a draft dodger and take him to a safe house. I remember the three of us stopped at a restaurant. The place was empty except for a group of older men sitting at a table near us. I heard one of them say, 'Look at those long-haired perverts. I bet they kidnapped that little girl.'"

T.S. watched as reactions claimed him. She watched his face turn the color of bleached flour and his eyes shutter his emotions. She watched him struggle for control and realized that he had been struggling to control hurtful childhood memories all his life.

"And the first time I watched television," he continued quietly, "I noticed how perfect families were depicted on those old shows like *Donna Reed*. Those fathers were never thrown in jail for civil disobedience or for desecrating the American flag. Those mothers wore pearls and white gloves, and they solved all their children's problems in half an hour. Those families never had the sheriff regularly coming by to check if they were growing pot in between the petunias and the pansies."

There was a short silence as Logan wearily passed his hand over his face. "I wanted to be the same as everybody else. I looked at my parents and the way they lived through the eyes of other people, and I was ashamed and embarrassed because we weren't one of those perfect TV families. So, I planned to create the person I wanted to be. Jack helped me. He changed the date of my birth certificate, making me two years older, and he changed my first name to my mother's maiden name, and he chose the surname 'Hunter' because he thought it was a great pun." Logan's gaze swung back to her for a moment. "To chase is to hunt—the hunter chases its prey. Jack had a warped sense of humor," he said wryly. "I took the GED, got my high school diploma, joined the navy, and—you know the rest."

He searched her face for some sign of support, for something positive, for anything to reassure him she wasn't condemning him. But all he found was T.S. deep in thought. Doubtful thought, it seemed to him. The emotions that had been unleashed inside him while telling his story combined with disappointment and rejection. He wrapped his arms around his legs, needing something to hold on to, needing something to subdue the hurt rising up inside him, needing something to steady the world that had come crashing down on him.

He closed his eyes, trying to swallow the lump of fear forming in his throat. Had he hurt her too badly for her to forgive?

Ten

T.S. bowed her head and plucked nervously at the sheet covering her breasts as she tried to digest everything Logan had told her. She had heard every imaginable reason for why children run away in search of a better life, some as simple as "My parents hassle me all the time," and some so horrific, she couldn't think of them without wanting to cry. But never had she been personally involved with one of those kids as she had been with Logan, in the past and the present. She cringed inside, thinking about what he had gone through and how emotionally damaged he had become as a result.

Thoughts churned wildly through her mind. When they had met as teenagers, she had been too caught up in her own misery to delve too deeply into his. Yet she remembered being curious about the sad expression that often haunted his eyes when he thought no one was looking. Now she knew what had made that boy slip into another identity as easily as one might slip into a pair of jeans. She filled in the blanks of the things he'd left unsaid, coloring them with the most hurtful shades, and she understood his need for a wall of fire.

When she lifted her head to look at him, she saw his waiting expression suddenly become unreadable. His eyelashes fanned down over his eyes. He was still hiding from her emotionally. That realization fed the anemic flame of anger still trapped inside her heart.

"Okay, I can understand. I can see what drove you to run away and why you felt the need to create a new life for yourself."

Holding himself aloof from the emotions rioting through him, Logan turned his wooden gaze to the window.

"What I don't understand," she went on, "is why you didn't trust me enough to tell me any of this freely. You said you cared about me. Did you lie about that too?"

He heard the reproach and hurt infused into her words. Nothing in his life had ever made him feel more powerless than he felt right now. A tiny smile edged the tight line of his mouth, but he still couldn't look at her. "I didn't lie about that. Distrust is deeply ingrained in me. I've had over sixteen years of practice."

T.S. narrowed her gaze. "Old habits are hard to break," she snapped. "Is that your excuse?" Her voice rose on the last word in an indignant squeak. "Well, I don't buy that, Moon Man, I mean Logan, I—" She struck the mattress with her fist in frustration. "I don't even know what to call you. I'm so confused."

"Maybe it isn't much of an excuse, but it's all I've got. I had come to believe the fictional middle-class background I had created for myself. When you reentered my life, I felt threatened." He shrugged. "Call me whatever suits you."

"Then I choose son of a—" She didn't complete the sentence, choosing instead to rein in her turbulent emotions. "How could I make you feel threatened? You know I would never do anything to intentionally harm you. I loved you sixteen years ago, and I fell in love with you all over again."

"I was trying to hold on to the illusion. But I couldn't hold. You made me face all the things I've been trying to forget. Moon Man was dead. You brought him back to life, and now—"

"Dammit, have the decency to look at me!" she interrupted furiously. "Stop hiding from me, Logan."

His eyes were bright as embers as he met her angry gaze. "I'm sorry, T.S. If I had it to do over again—"

"You'd probably do the same thing," she said bitterly. "Don't lie to either of us about that. You've betrayed me twice. Once for money and once for this damn fantasy you've created."

"No!" he almost shouted. "I admit I called your father to come get you. But I *never* asked him for money. He just handed me a wad of hundred-dollar bills. And I also admit I was tempted, very tempted to keep it. Then I looked at you and saw the pain in your eyes. I felt physically ill. I gave the money back to your father."

"You took it. I saw you!"

"Call your father and ask him, if you don't believe me. You didn't see me return his money because you had already turned your back on me." He lowered his voice. "And you never looked at me again."

T.S. didn't want to believe him, but she did. "I loved you," she whispered. "You hurt me." She wanted to hold tight to her anger and disillusionment, but it was becoming increasingly difficult for her.

Logan's heart contracted painfully. He took a long, unsteady breath. "When we met, I saw you as an innocent, tragic-eyed princess, and I wanted to protect you, keep you safe from harm. Somewhere along the way, I began to care deeply about you. Maybe it was because you didn't laugh at me."

He smiled, and it was a new smile, one she'd never seen grace his hard, unyielding face. It was breathtakingly soft, and it reached out to touch her like the most loving caress.

"Maybe it was watching you sitting on the counter in the kitchen of Jack's tiny apartment. I can still see you fresh out of the shower with your hair cascading down your back. You just sat there, kicking your heels, smiling, and watching me with hero worship in your beautiful blue eyes. And damned if I didn't feel like one. No one had ever looked at me the way you did."

He moved to sit in front of her. His hands rested on her shoulders, then fell to his sides when she jerked away. "Every night I lay awake, sweating and waiting for morning because I wanted you so badly. Every night I heard you crying in your sleep, and it was heartbreaking. I'd get up and kneel beside the bed and stroke your hair until you stopped crying. Then I'd stay there for hours, watching you sleep, needing you, wanting something I couldn't have."

She was stunned by the image of him kneeling beside her bed, giving comfort and asking for none in return. The sheet dropped from her trembling fingers and fell to her waist.

"I contacted your father because I cared about what happened to you."

"You did love me," she whispered. "Then why did you never kiss me until that last day? I wanted you, needed you. I would have given you anything—my body, my heart, my soul." Tears glistened like blue diamonds in her eyes.

He touched her face. With the tips of his fingers, in a long-ago gesture his heart remembered only too well, he caught the tears seeping from her eyes as they slowly rolled down her cheeks. His voice as gentle as his touch, he said, "Don't you think I know you would have welcomed me into your body? I couldn't, T.S., I just couldn't."

She strained away from him. Her tensed hands went limp. She opened her mouth to speak but could say nothing.

Logan held himself with rigid control. "You were too young. We both were. I had nothing to offer you but the future I planned to base on lies. And I think in some crazy way, I believed I had given up the right to love and be loved when I ruthlessly walked away from the people who loved me."

T.S. felt her heart shattering into a million pieces. He'd shown her love, compassion, and vulnerability, mixed with pain and needs of his own that had gone unfulfilled for half of his lifetime.

Tears streamed down her face as she got to her knees, rising above him. Her hands dived into his hair, and she tilted his head back so she could see his face, see his eyes.

"I can't even begin to imagine the pain of feeling unworthy of giving and receiving love. Oh, Logan, you're so wrong." Her voice broke on a sob. "When you're young and people hurt you, it changes the way you look at the world, and sometimes it distorts your view of yourself."

She bent to kiss his lips, softly, briefly. "Nothing, *nothing* you have done, past or present, makes you unlovable. Love isn't earned. It's given freely."

Blood pounded in Logan's head, in his heart, in every part of his body. She had just given him a second miracle. An unexpected, unanticipated, unexplainable miracle.

Her hands dug into his shoulders. "I've felt hurt by you. I've felt betrayed by you." With the palm of one hand she lightly shoved him. "I'm mad as hell at you for so many things."

Suddenly, she released him and dropped down on her heels. "Don't you understand how valuable it is to know that someone on this chaotic planet loves you? And I *do* love you. You're *free* to love me back if you want to. If you can honestly tell me you love me, I can begin to forgive."

Eyes brimming with tears, he struggled to say the words that were so hard for him to speak aloud. His heart thundered. A sweat broke out on his brow. "I—I," he whispered. In a stronger voice he started again. "T.S., I love you. I always have. I always will. I want a chance to make things right. Will you give me that chance?"

Stiffening her spine, T.S. fought the desire to melt into his arms. "There can be no more lies between us, Logan. No more hiding. I want everything from you—emotionally, physically, spiritually. I want to share your past, present, and future. I will not settle for less. Are you willing to give me what I want?"

Hope swelled within his chest. His heart in his throat, he said, "I'll do my best. It isn't easy for me to share those parts of myself, but I want to with you. You'll have to help me learn how."

She nodded, not trusting herself to speak but pouring everything she felt into a blindingly radiant smile.

Logan reached for her, wanting to hold the love, the forgiveness, the salvation she offered.

They fell onto the bed in a tangle of frenzied need. They came together, lips meeting and parting, hands touching palm to palm, whispering words of love and desire.

He caught her dreamy sigh with his mouth as he entered her softness. Then every part of him was engulfed in her as he thrust himself fully into her. He closed his eyes in wonder, in reverent worship, of the love he felt welling up inside him. And the words "I love you," which had been so hard for him to say, spilling joyfully from his mouth time after time.

Afterward, they held each other close and talked of the way things should be, of joining their lives together in marriage to share all of life's possibilities, all its opportunities; of compassion and compromise, of no more hiding and hurting from the past.

When Logan told her of his decision to go home to Freedom Farm, she sought his mouth in a lingering kiss full of warmth, promise, and loving support. She praised him for the courageous step he'd taken in making that decision.

"I know it won't be easy for you," she said softly.

"But I'll be there for you. Together we can get through anything."

He stroked her hair. "I want to give you the Greensboro property for the shelter."

"You don't have to do that," she protested.

"I want to. You've given me back my ability to care and to feel not only for myself but for others. Take the building. Consider it a wedding present. T.S., I honestly want to give it to you for All Saints."

She smiled because she saw the truth of it in his eyes. "I'll take it. And every time a child walks through the door of the shelter, I'll remember how you helped me, and how I came to love you."

Someone was crying.

Jesse awoke with a start. Eyes blinking adjustment to the dark, he lay very still. Groggy and confused, he didn't know at first what had woken him.

Someone was crying. His spine stiffened in shock as he realized it was he. He lifted his hand in disbelief and touched his wet face, feeling the first tears to fall from his eyes in—he couldn't remember how long it had been. Years, he guessed.

Fear suddenly grabbed him with icy fingers. If he could cry, he could feel. He could be hurt.

The trembling started in his legs and worked its way up to his lips. Great, pain-filled sobs racked his small body. It was a hurtful sound, a broken, wounded sound. Covering his ears, he sat up and scooted back into the corner.

Minutes later, when he was all cried out, Jesse knew what he had to do, what he needed to do.

He lowered his hands to the concrete floor and pushed himself up. On shaky legs he walked to the door and opened it. Pallid morning light rushed into the storage room and blinded him for a moment.

Taking a deep, shuddering breath, he ran out to the gravel-and shell-strewn road, racing toward her cottage.

They had just finished making breakfast when they heard a timid knocking at the door.

Logan grinned at T.S. "If that's Mrs. Midgett coming to find out why I failed to show up at work without calling, you handle her. That woman scares me to death."

T. S. patted his cheek. "Poor baby, don't worry. I'll protect you from your big, bad secretary." She laughed when he swatted her on the behind and went to answer the door.

"Mamie's all bark and no bite," she called after him. "Under her left D-cup beats a mushy heart."

"Yeah, right," he growled as he pulled the door open. His eyes widened with surprise when he saw the boy. "Well, good morning."

"I—I'm sorry to bother you," Jesse stammered. "But I was looking for T.S." He lowered his gaze and stared at the toes of his scruffy sneakers. "She's not home. I thought, well, since she said you were her friend, you might know where she is."

Logan stood back and opened the door wide enough for the child to see into the room. "Please come in. T.S. is here. I know she'll be glad to see you. We were just about to eat breakfast. I hope you'll join us. We made enough eggs and toast to feed a small army."

The boy raised his head and searched the man's face for the kindness he heard in his voice. "Thank you," he whispered, and walked across the threshold.

THE EDITOR'S CORNER

Next month LOVESWEPT brings you spirited heroines and to-die-for heroes in stories that explore romance in all its forms—sensuous, sweet, heartwarming, and funny. And the title of each novel is so deliciously compelling, you won't know which one to read first.

There's no better way to describe Gavin Magadan than as a **LEAN MEAN LOVING MACHINE,** LOVESWEPT #546, by Sandra Chastain, for in his boots and tight jeans he is one dangerously handsome hunk. And Stacy Lanham has made a bet to vamp him! How can she play the seducer when she's much better at replacing spark plugs than setting off sparks? Gavin shows her the way, though, when he lets himself be charmed by the lady whose lips he yearns to kiss. Sandra has created a winner with this enthralling story.

In **SLOW BURN,** LOVESWEPT #547, by Cindy Gerard, passion heats to a boiling point between Joanna Taylor and Adam Dursky. When he takes on the job of handyman in her lodge, she's drawn to a loneliness in him that echoes her own, and she longs for his strong embrace with a fierce desire. Can a redheaded rebel who's given up on love heal the pain of a tough renegade? The intensity of Cindy's writing makes this a richly emotional tale you'll long remember.

In Linda Jenkins's newest LOVESWEPT, #548, Sam Wonder *is* **MR. WONDERFUL,** a heart-stopping combination of muscles and cool sophistication. But he's furious when Trina Bartok shows up at his Ozarks resort, convinced she's just the latest candidate in his father's endless matchmaking. Still, he can't deny the sensual current that crackles between them, and when Trina makes it clear she's there only for a temporary job, he resolves to make her a permanent part of his life. Be sure not to miss this treat from Linda.

dy Gill's offering for the month, **SUMMER LOVER,** OVESWEPT #549, will have you thinking summer may be the most romantic season of all—although romance is the furthest thing from Donna Mailer's mind when she goes to Gray Kincaid's office to refuse his offer to buy her uncle's failing campground business. After all, the Kincaid family nearly ruined her life. But Gray's passionate persuasion soon has her sweetly surrendering amid tangled sheets. Judy's handling of this story is nothing less than superb.

Most LOVESWEPTs end with the hero and heroine happily deciding to marry, but Olivia Rupprecht, who has quickly developed a reputation for daring to be different, begins **I DO!,** #550, with Sol Standish in the Middle East and Mariah Garnett in the Midwest exchanging wedding vows through the telephone—and that's before they ever lay eyes on each other. When they finally come face-to-face, will their innocent love survive the test of harsh reality? Olivia will take your breath away with this original and stunning romance.

INTIMATE VIEW by Diane Pershing, LOVESWEPT #551, will send you flying in a whirlwind of exquisite sensation. Ben Kane certainly feels that way when he glimpses a goddess rising naked from the ocean. He resented being in a small California town to run a cable franchise until he sees Nell Pritchard and she fires his blood—enough to make him risk the danger of pursuing the solitary spitfire whose sanctuary he's invaded. Diane's second LOVE-SWEPT proves she's one of the finest newcomers to the genre.

On sale this month from FANFARE are three marvelous novels. The historical romance **HEATHER AND VELVET** showcases the exciting talent of a rising star—Teresa Medeiros. Her marvelous touch for creating memorable characters and her exquisite feel for portraying passion and emotion shine in this grand adventure of love between a bookish orphan and a notorious highwayman known as the Dreadful Scot Bandit. Ranging from the storm-swept English countryside to the wild moors of Scotland, **HEATHER AND VELVET** has garnered the following praise from *New York Times* bestselling author Amanda Quick: "A terrific tale full of larger-than-life characters and thrilling romance." Teresa Medeiros—a name to watch for.

Lush, dramatic, and poignant, **LADY HELLFIRE,** by Suzanne Robinson, is an immensely thrilling historical romance. Its hero, Alexis de Granville, Marquess of Richfield, is a cold-blooded rogue whose tragic—and possibly violent—past has hardened his heart to love . . . until he melts at the fiery touch of Kate Grey's sensual embrace.

Anna Eberhardt, whose short romances have been published under the pseudonym Tiffany White, has been nominated for *Romantic Times*'s Career Achievement award for Most Sensual Romance in a series. Now she delivers **WHISPERED HEAT,** a compelling contemporary novel of love lost, then regained. When Slader Reems is freed after five years of being wrongly imprisoned, he sets out to reclaim everything that was taken from him—including Lissa Jamison.

Also on sale this month, in the Doubleday hardcover edition, is **LIGHTNING,** by critically acclaimed Patricia Potter. During the Civil War, nobody was a better Confederate blockade runner than Englishman Adrian Cabot, but Lauren Bradley swore to stop him. Together they would be swept into passion's treacherous sea, tasting deeply of ecstasy and the danger of war.

Happy reading!

With warmest wishes,

Nita Taublib
Associate Publisher
LOVESWEPT and FANFARE

FANFARE

Now On Sale
THE FIREBIRDS

☐ 29613-2 $4.99/5.99 in Canada
by Beverly Byrne
author of THE MORGAN WOMEN

The third and final book in Beverly Byrne's remarkable trilogy of passion and revenge. The fortunes of the House of Mendoza are stunningly resolved in this contemporary romance.

FORTUNE'S CHILD

☐ 29424-5 $5.99/6.99 in Canada
by Pamela Simpson

Twenty years ago, Christina Fortune disappeared. Now she's come home to claim what's rightfully hers. But is she an heiress . . . or an imposter?

SEASON OF SHADOWS

☐ 29589-6 $5.99/6.99 in Canada
by Mary Mackey

Lucy and Cassandra were polar opposites, but from the first day they met they became the best of friends. Roommates during the turbulent sixties, they stood beside each other through fiery love affairs and heartbreaking loneliness.

FANFARE

Rosanne Bittner

_____ 28599-8 EMBERS OF THE HEART . $4.50/5.50 in Canada
_____ 29033-9 IN THE SHADOW OF THE MOUNTAINS
$5.50/6.99 in Canada
_____ 28319-7 MONTANA WOMAN .... $4.50/5.50 in Canada
_____ 29014-2 SONG OF THE WOLF .... $4.99/5.99 in Canada

Deborah Smith

_____ 28759-1 THE BELOVED WOMAN .. $4.50/ 5.50 in Canada
_____ 29092-4 FOLLOW THE SUN .... $4.99/ 5.99 in Canada
_____ 29107-6 MIRACLE .... $4.50/ 5.50 in Canada

Tami Hoag

_____ 29053-3 MAGIC .... $3.99/4.99 in Canada

Dianne Edouard and Sandra Ware

_____ 28929-2 MORTAL SINS .... $4.99/5.99 in Canada

Kay Hooper

_____ 29256-0 THE MATCHMAKER, ... $4.50/5.50 in Canada
_____ 28953-5 STAR-CROSSED LOVERS .. $4.50/5.50 in Canada

Virginia Lynn

_____ 29257-9 CUTTER'S WOMAN, ... $4.50/4.50 in Canada
_____ 28622-6 RIVER'S DREAM, ... $3.95/4.95 in Canada

Patricia Potter

_____ 29071-1 LAWLESS .... $4.99/ 5.99 in Canada
_____ 29069-X RAINBOW .... $4.99/ 5.99 in Canada

Ask for these titles at your bookstore or use this page to order.

Please send me the books I have checked above. I am enclosing $ _____ (please add $2.50 to cover postage and handling). Send check or money order, no cash or C. O. D.'s please.

Mr./ Ms. _____

Address _____

City/ State/ Zip _____

Send order to: Bantam Books, Dept. FN, 414 East Golf Road, Des Plaines, IL 60016
Please allow four to six weeks for delivery.
Prices and availablity subject to change without notice.   FN 17 - 4/92